As Long as
There are Trees

by

Norma LaFleur

Bloomington, IN   authorHOUSE™   Milton Keynes, UK

AuthorHouse™
1663 Liberty Drive, Suite 200
Bloomington, IN 47403
www.authorhouse.com
Phone: 1-800-839-8640

AuthorHouse™ UK Ltd.
500 Avebury Boulevard
Central Milton Keynes, MK9 2BE
www.authorhouse.co.uk
Phone: 08001974150

This story is a work of fiction. Any reference to historical events, to real people, living or dead, or to real locales, establishments or events is intended only to give the fiction a setting in historical reality. Other names, characters, places, and incidents are the product of the author's imagination or are used fictitiously, and their resemblance, if any, to real-life counterparts is entirely coincidental.

First published by AuthorHouse 5/18/2006

ISBN: 1-4259-2314-3 (sc)

Printed in the United States of America
Bloomington, Indiana

This book is printed on acid-free paper.

Grateful acknowledgement is made to the Arthur Waley Estate for permission to quote from Arthur Waley's translation of Shikibu Murasaki's "A Wreath of Cloud" from "The Tale of Genji" Houghton Mifflin Company, Boston & New York, 1927: pp. 253-254. (First published by G. Allen & Unwin Ltd., London, 1927.)

And for permission to quote from Arthur Waley's translation of "The Lady Who Loved Insects" Blackamore Press, London, 1929. (Later published in "The Real Tripitaka and Other Pieces" G. Allen & Unwin Ltd., 1952.)

Library of Congress Control Number: 2006902179

For Jeanne Marie and David

Epigraph

One day Genji, going the round with a number of romances which he had promised to lend, came to Tamakatsura's room and found her as usual, hardly able to lift her eyes from the book in front of her. "Really, you are incurable," he said, laughing. "I sometimes think that young ladies exist for no other purpose than to provide purveyors of the absurd and improbable with a market for their wares. I am sure that the book you are now so intent upon is full of the wildest nonsense. Yet knowing this all the time, you are completely captivated by its extravagances and follow them with the utmost excitement: why, here you are on this hot day, so hard at work that, though I am sure you have not the least idea of it, your hair is in the most extraordinary tangle....But there; I know quite well that these old tales are indispensable during such weather as this. How else would you manage to get through the day? Now for a confession. I too have lately been studying these books and have, I must tell you, been amazed by the delight which they have given me. There is, it seems, an art of so fitting each part of the narrative into the next that, though all is mere invention, the reader is persuaded that such things might easily have happened and is as deeply moved as though they were actually going on around him. We may know with one part of our minds that every incident has been invented for the express purpose of impressing us; but (if the plot is constructed with the requisite skill) we may all the while in another part of our minds be burning with indignation at the wrongs endured by some wholly imaginary princess. Or again we may be persuaded by a writer's eloquence into accepting the crudest absurdities, our judgment being as it were dazzled by sheer splendour of the language.

"A Wreath of Cloud" Being the third Part of "The Tale of Genji" by Lady Murasaki. Translated from the Japanese by Arthur Waley, Houghton Mifflin Company, 1927, pp. 253-254 (first published by G. Allen & Unwin Ltd., London, 1927).

Sunday, August 2, 1970. California is no longer visible below. We are flying north to touchdown in Anchorage before continuing on over the Pacific to Japan. In the seat behind me, a man is snoring. Of all the passengers I noticed boarding the plane, this man alone carried no book or newspaper or briefcase or bag to store in an overhead bin. He fastened his seatbelt, pulled the shade down over the window, sandwiched himself between a pillow and a blanket, and fell asleep, possibly with the intention of sleeping all the way to Japan. Others, like me, are looking for distractions. The plane is not crowded. After we were airborne, the businessman sitting beside me asked the stewardess if she could move him to a row of empty seats in the back near the lavatories where he could work throughout the night without disturbing me.

I stretched out over his vacated seat and mine and alternated between staring out the window and thumbing through fashion magazines Aunt Elizabeth bought for me at the airport, but clothes can't hold my interest. Starting my diary now instead of waiting until I get to Kyoto is a better way to control the mix of anxiety and confidence I have carried on board.

Being awarded an Asuka Foundation grant to work with Professor Hiraizumi, a Buddhist art scholar at Kyoto University, on an English translation of a nobleman's diary called *Mountain Temple Woman* boosted my confidence. I wrote to Professor Hiraizumi the day after I read his article about the diary in an Asian art periodical to ask if anyone had contacted him about translating it into English. No, he replied, he had not received other inquiries about a translation, and, yes, he welcomed my interest in coming to Kyoto within the next year as he planned to retire the following year and would be giving up his office at the university.

Experienced translators who might have read the professor's article must not have found it interesting enough to question why a nobleman would take time to record his conversations with a well-born elderly woman whose life was not unusual for that time in Japanese history. Who better than a female scholar like me willing to work in solitude, for the most part, to translate an otherwise anonymous woman's life?

1

I applied for the Asuka Foundation grant right away, and in subsequent letters, Professor Hiraizumi told me he would make his collection of supporting materials available to me (the collection includes rare and out-of-print letters and articles that he has been adding to, buying when necessary, over the years). He also gave me the name and address of the person responsible for managing the apartments adjacent to Kyoto University, which were available to foreign scholars and visiting fellows.

What surprised and delighted me most was how readily Professor Hiraizumi responded to my directness with his own brand of directness in agreeing to facilitate my work on the translation. With only two years of teaching experience and just two published articles, my curriculum vitae is not impressive.

The first time I wrote to him, my thesis was a book-in-press and several more weeks had to pass before I could send him a published copy.

I am interested in the portrayal of women's lives in literature. My doctoral thesis in comparative literature began taking shape after I'd completed my undergraduate degree in Japanese history and while living independently in Tokyo instead of on an army base with my aunt and uncle. I had found a copy of Arthur Waley's (Blackamore Press, London, 1929) translation of *The Lady Who Loved Insects* in a puddle on the floor of a second-hand bookstore in Ueno. It must have been knocked from the shelf by someone as intent as I was in finding shelter from a thunderstorm, someone who unknowingly let their umbrella drip on the fallen book while thumbing through another book that caught their eye.

This lady's story is one of ten in a collection of short stories written during the late Heian Period (794 to possibly 1194) and the one Mr. Waley so beautifully translated. Reading the story gave me the confidence I needed to leave Japanese history to work toward a doctorate in comparative literature. I know this part of Mr. Waley's translation by heart, "I do not mind what they (neighbors who judge her) think, I want to inquire into everything that exists and find out how it began. Nothing else interests me. And it is very silly of them to dislike caterpillars, all of which will soon turn into lovely butterflies."

Stories circulate about her interest in caterpillars. Young men in her neighborhood consider her a "disastrous character." A certain young man of good family plays a trick on her by sending her an authentic-looking toy snake that sets her ladies-in-waiting in a dither. And later, when he knew her father wasn't around, a certain Captain of the Horse hid behind a gate made of wattle to get a closer look at her. He could see she didn't blacken her teeth with a cosmetic, which was the custom of the day, and paid little attention to her long, trailing hair.

"What a sad case," thought the captain. "If only she took an ordinary amount of trouble with herself, she really would not be bad-looking." And continuing to quote Mr. Waley, "But even as she was, he did not find her altogether unattractive; for there was about her a strange kind of vehemence and authority, a liveliness of expression, a brilliancy of complexion and colouring that could not fail to make some impression on him."

When her maid expressed her dismay, the lady said, "If you looked a little more below the surface of things, you would not mind so much what people thought about you. The world in which we live has no reality: it is a mirage, a dream. Suppose someone is offended by what we do, or, for the matter of that, is pleased by it, does his opinion make any difference to us in the end? Before long both he and we shall no longer even appear to exist."

The lady had been carefully brought up to know the standard of behavior expected from well-born women and girls, and she had to live and deal with these expectations in a reasonable manner. I was drawn to her story by my own desire for meaningful study. I, too, wanted to see what lies beyond the shape of things, what reveals itself when we explore the text.

After reading her story several times, I went back to the bookstore and bought two volumes of Mr. Waley's translation of *The Tale of Genji* to reread and review. Substantial ideas for my doctoral thesis grew out of this focused reading period, and I saved these ideas in a notebook. In the late 1960s, after I'd finished my thesis, I was fortunate to find a publisher alert to the growing interest in questions and answers women were voicing about their contributions to literature, history, science, etc. etc.

3

The title of my book, *Romances of an Old Order: Stories from the Heian Period,* was chosen by my editor with the hope of enticing interest in the lives of these women. Not much interest was generated, although initial reviews were good. Having it published soon after I received my doctorate supported my candidacy for a teaching position at Southern Women's College, and later, when I applied for an Asuka grant, I hoped the foundation officers reviewing my application would overlook the title and search for substance within the contents of the book.

No job is waiting for me when I return from Japan, but I am hoping I'll have one or two good prospects by then. Mother thinks I should stay home and look for a job in California. "Oh, no, not again," is her usual response when I tell her I'm leaving the States. I told her my translation would support future job applications and add another book to my CV. Once she'd resigned herself to my leaving, we reconciled by planning what I would take on the plane or send ahead and what I might possibly need during the winter months. After that, she called Aunt Elizabeth and Uncle Arthur to arrange today's unified sendoff at the airport.

I'm depending on Professor Smith, my thesis advisor and friend, to help me find a job after I return. She pulled a rabbit out of the hat when she found a position for me at Southern Women's College. We both scrambled after the two jobs in California for which I had interviewed went to other candidates. She called the department chair at SWC until he relented and agreed to interview me for the two-year position they advertised. It was difficult for him to imagine a California grad as a suitable candidate for a women's college in the Deep South because of what he had read about the Haight-Ashbury Love Movement, all those flower children and anti-draft rallies; nevertheless, he listened to Dr. Smith's repeated assurances about my being a serious student with an upright, moral character and modest deportment, telling him I had been raised in a small town in northern California by both my parents and grandparents, until, his defenses worn away by her persistence, he granted me an interview. I didn't mind being made to sound prim and proper if that's what it took to get the job.

Dr. Smith told me to put aside my disappointment in not finding a job in California and to think positively about the teaching experience I would gain if the position were offered because there are students at every college who make teaching worthwhile. It was up to me to find those at SWC who would make my work there challenging and worthwhile.

Her advice for winning the position was to be myself, wear my long braids in a crown in lieu of a hat, to wear either a floral-patterned dress and jacket or a soft-colored linen dress if the weather was especially warm and to carry white gloves. This combination, she said, would make a favorable impression on the department chair, a man born and bred in the South. She was right; he offered me a contract before my return flight to California.

That first year at SWC, I was more homesick than I remembered being during my freshman year in college or while studying in Japan. I relied on long telephone conversations with my parents and Aunt Elizabeth to help me find secure ground. Two female colleagues, both single and graduates of SWC before earning doctorates elsewhere in science and literature, became helpful, supportive friends. It was through them I learned that until five years ago, married women were offered only part-time contracts with no benefits. Married or unmarried, women professors are still paid less than married or unmarried male professors, and taking care of a physically disabled and dependent parent for fifteen years, as one of my friends had done, was not considered reason enough to equalize the pay scale.

My contract with SWC stipulated I live in the freshman dorm as assistant dorm supervisor. My main responsibility was to be sure the girls signed out when they left for a weekend at home. Sunday evening, they signed in carrying hampers of food and gave me tasty samples of cold fried chicken, some of the best I have eaten, Sally Lunn, hushpuppies, okra and tomatoes, fried dill pickles, delicious ham, and biscuits.

It wasn't unusual for a freshman to come back wearing her boyfriend's fraternity pin, relieved, it seemed to me, to have the big question of what to do after college settled during a weekend at home. Other girls left college after their first semester or the end of their freshman year to marry. I thought cutting short their education was a mistake and said so when asked during a conversation in the lounge. Still, their rush to marry had me rethinking my decision not to marry until I was well established in my career.

At SWC, I learned that being a well-bred Southern lady meant one strove to be gracious, resilient, loyal, courageous in the face of hardship, self-sacrificing when circumstances require such an offering, reticent about revealing or discussing personal problems, aware of her family's place in the social hierarchy, consistent in habits of good grooming and proper conduct, and hopeful of making an advantageous marriage. It was similar to what I knew about the ladies of the Heian Court, and I used it to introduce these two groups of ladies to each other. Thoughtful, insightful class discussions encouraged me in my efforts, and several students' papers had me probing deeper into assigned texts and my own assumptions and conclusions. Teaching was teaching me far more than I could have anticipated.

This coming year in Japan will be the first time I have had to depend entirely on voiceless sheets of white paper to catch the unpredictable flow of homesickness as well as absorb leftovers from work and the letters I write home. I'll have to manage the days ahead with just this diary to record the impressions I gather during walks around the city. The conversations I have with Professor Hiraizumi will be absorbed in my work on the translation. Telling the butcher I want 50 or 100 grams of chicken fillet or handing over the correct amount of yen for the tangerines I buy at the greengrocer will not be worth recording, and I'll probably run out of things to write about before I reach the end of this diary.

For my first trip to Japan in 1956, my parents gave me a leather-bound diary. I was fourteen, almost fifteen and, like me, none of my friends had traveled overseas. I loved telling them I was going abroad to spend the summer with my aunt and uncle. It had the ring of sophistication, but Japan was not high on the list of countries my friends wanted to visit even ten years after World War II. To my group of friends, going abroad meant spending time in France, England, or Italy as these countries were known from what we'd learned about our ancestors and from what we studied in school. Announcing my intention of spending the summer in Japan was an opportunity for my friends to talk about their hopes for trips to Paris, Rome, Florence, or Venice, and nobody got around to asking about my upcoming trip to Japan.

My parents were surprised to have a daughter who was eager to travel because they were homebodies who thought Red Oak, California was the best place to live. Our family vacations were spent at camping sites in California, which was exciting when I was growing up and too young to consider being on my own. I am the only child of parents who had me when they were both forty and had given up hope of having a child of their own. I lived with both my parents and grandparents in the house my grandfather had built, and I shall always be grateful to the four of them, as well as Aunt Elizabeth and Uncle Arthur, for all the intangibly good things they've given me besides my name, brown eyes, and brown hair.

My mother went to San Francisco after high school to study bookkeeping and economics and came home to manage the financial arm of my grandfather's woodworking and furniture business. She has been content living in Red Oak. Aunt Elizabeth, my mother's younger sister, never had children and passed through her early forties without a surprise pregnancy. She is my godmother in fact as well as in the fairy-tale sense of direction and opportunity. She says she's always known she wanted to travel and see the world. Shortly after Aunt Elizabeth moved to San Francisco to take a job, she met and married Uncle Arthur who had chosen the military as his career. She has accompanied him to most of his postings except during much of World War II, yet even if she hadn't married Uncle Arthur, she would have traveled to countries whose art and culture she admired and studied. She has that kind of independence.

In the early part of the summer in 1956, she was in California looking for a house in San Francisco where she and Uncle Arthur wanted to live when he retired from the Army, and she set about convincing my parents it was safe to let me spend the summer in Japan. I remember her telling my parents, "It's 1956; the war with Japan is over, and the Korean War is finished for now. What major mishap could befall Marina while living on an army base with two competent adults and the American Army to look after her?"

Although my 1956 diary does go on a bit much about the girls I met on base, the most interesting part to me now is my trip to Yamanashi Prefecture to spend ten days in the country with the Nakamura family. Uncle Arthur wanted me to see and experience more of Japan than what I was absorbing from shopping trips into Tokyo with Aunt Elizabeth and brief sightseeing trips. He will not tell me how he was able to arrange this and changes the subject whenever I've asked. The stated purpose of those ten days was to help sixteen-year-old Yuriko Nakamura with English conversation.

We two girls struggled with Japanese and English and relied heavily on our intuition as well as charades and her ability to quickly draw objects that helped us understand what the other was trying to say. Her tutoring helped me express my thanks to her parents in Japanese the last day of my visit when we gathered in the large *tatami* room to say our formal farewell. Yuriko-san also taught me how to make a summer kimono, a *yukata* that has become a reminder of my trip to Yamanashi Prefecture and those hot summer days we spent talking and sewing in the *tatami* room where the family formally received guests, and which we two girls converted into a bedroom at night.

It's apparent from my diary how wonderfully ordinary I thought everything was. Eating every meal with *hashi* (chopsticks) instead of knives and forks was different, not exotic. I did have to prove I could manage eating with *hashi* before Mrs. Nakamura stopped offering me a spoon with my meals. We sat on cushions around a low table instead of at a high table with chairs. We ate three meals a day, washed the dishes, had tea and snacks, laundered our own underwear, took walks around the fields and a longer walk to the three stores near the bus stop, sewed new clothing and mended old garments, and mopped the hallway every day because the sliding doors were left wide open and dust floated into the house and onto the dark wood in the hallway, as well as everyplace else. I was used to helping with housework at home, but I had to convince Yuriko-san I was qualified to help clean her house, and she, finally—it was really Mr. Nakamura who had the final say—let me help with her chores. We had fun when we bent over with our hips raised and raced down the hallway pushing damp cloths ahead of us until the individual boards shone like strips of dark brown satin.

Of course, there were deeper, more abiding cultural differences I didn't grasp at the time and nuances I couldn't pick up as I didn't have the cultural wherewithal to understand; nevertheless, that brief stay with the Nakamura's provided me with a familiarity and taste for things Japanese that continues to enrich my studies.

Yuriko-san had two older brothers we saw mostly at meals because they both worked in the fields with their father. The youngest boy was a spoiled ten-year-old I called Godzilla-chan (child) in my diary. He could be a monster at times, but he could also be quite charming and funny. It was all so similar to what I knew at home when I stayed overnight with girlfriends who had a younger brother or sister.

Having me around made Mrs. Nakamura uncomfortable. It had not been easy to convince her a foreigner in her home could be a benign presence. Mr. Nakamura had had the deciding vote, and he voted for the added benefit I could bring to his daughter's education over the inconvenience of housing a foreign girl who did not speak Japanese and had to learn how to live in a Japanese-style house. Mr. Nakamura was a short, squat, judicious man, who cared a great deal for his children, and he had a voiceless way of conveying his approval or disapproval that even I—a stranger and foreigner—could read. He and Mrs. Nakamura rarely spoke to each other while I was around. The few times they sat together on the narrow verandah outside the *tatami* room, he leaned his head toward hers and apparently meaning and intention leaped across the narrow space between them.

Every night, Yuriko-san and I converted the large, open *tatami* room we used for family meals, my sewing lessons, and where her parents formally received guests and visitors. When it was time for bed, we two girls converted it into our bedroom by closing all the sliding doors, pushing the low table into a corner, and spreading our two futons in the center with a small lamp in between. Together, we took our turn in the *ofuro* where we soaked in deep, hot water and practiced English and Japanese conversation and were often giddy from mistakes and mispronunciations. Back in our bedroom, we stretched out on futons to write in our diaries. Her diary was vacation homework she would give to her teacher after she returned to school.

Yuriko-san put aside her usual modesty to tell me she would have the most interesting diary in her class because of my visit. Apparently, she didn't have much to say about it because she stopped writing and fell asleep long before I did.

At the end of my visit, while Yuriko-san and I were standing apart from her father on the station platform waiting for my train to Tokyo, she gave me the diary I am using this year. When I marveled at its brocade cover with stylized patterns of arched bridges and iris ponds, she told me, "It is a book of opportunity, Marina-san. Use it well."

By the end of that summer, I knew I wanted to return to Japan sometime in the future, and I decided to major in Japanese history instead of American history when I went to college. This surprised my parents who were proud, and rightly so, of our American heritage and our English, Irish, and Norman ancestors. They could not understand why I wanted to study the history of a country with whom we had so recently had to go to war, and the feeble explanations I attempted did not satisfy them.

It was a mistake to dedicate myself to the study of Japanese history, a subject in which I was totally ignorant, without first trying something else, but at fourteen, almost fifteen, I wanted clear, definable goals; I had to know then what I was going to study in college. It would take a long time, almost three years of college, before I had the courage and clarity to see, say, and act upon what was a better fit for my nature and interests—literature.

When I was a senior in high school taking honors English, my exceptional teacher's insights into literature pulled back the curtain covering my life and gave me another glimpse of what the future might possibly hold for me. In Miss Graves' class, lectures became a kind of mortar that brought my own reading and insights together with the text. In a paper I wrote for her class on the theme of journeying and discovery, I stated that both "In the beginning was the Word..." and "Once upon a time..." were encapsulations of the beginning of a journey of discovery that could result in understanding and peace. I knew little about the rigors of such a journey as I had no life experience to speak of and only a hazy vision of the kind of peace or the discoveries I hoped to make in life, but the word "encapsulation" gave me a heady feeling of empowerment while I was writing that paper.

While under the spell of one of Miss Graves' insightful lectures about the treasures in literature that can open a more meaningful life, I rushed to my guidance counselor's office, also my world history teacher, to tell him I had changed my mind, I now wanted to study literature in college instead of Japanese history. Sometime earlier, when I had met him in the hall and told him Miss Graves' awesome lecture on fairy tales had changed my life, he warned me against ecstatic gamboling, knowing the word "ecstatic" would tone down my enthusiasm to a more levelheaded approach, and his negative tone surrounding "gamboling" would send me to a dictionary to discover what was wrong in my declaration.

In almost every history class, he told us how we needed to be reasonable and levelheaded in our approach to the problems we would face in life. If we used reason, he assured us, we would succeed in whatever we decided to do. We knew he was right about a levelheaded approach to problems because as the school's football coach, he had led our team to the Northern State High School Championship two years in a row. During football season, he could be persuaded to take time from class to demonstrate the plays that had helped our team win a recent game. The majority of us thought he was an outstanding example of an energetic, involved, levelheaded teacher who offered practical advice. Twice, we dedicated the school yearbook to him.

During that particular visit to the guidance office, I felt obligated to tell him I wanted to change my college major. I jumped into my story with an exuberance that surprised me. The possibilities I saw in a career devoted to literature poured out in a deluge of excitement until he covered his face with his hands as if to ward off further demonstration of how he had failed as my teacher. My narration of adolescent leaps and bounds toward discovering what life could hold for me wearied him. According to what he had taught us, I was incoherently gamboling and could not be dealt with until I had calmed down and could listen to reason.

I knew he thought football, with its predictable rules, clearly defined goal posts, high soaring goals, and cheering crowds of students and parents safely confined to the bleachers was a healthier way to exhaust himself than fending off my ever-changing and often exalted view of what the future held for me. Speaking slowly and deliberately, as if I had difficulty understanding English, he enunciated every word, "Marina, fiction is cotton candy. Being an avid reader and loving the books you read will not make you a scholar. Women who study English in college are only biding time until they marry. (Miss Graves was over forty and unmarried.) They are lightweights. They never become serious scholars. (She had a master's degree in literature and attended graduate seminars during the summer.) History is a true record of what has happened; it tells how people lived and died, what they said and did. It is meat for serious scholarship. You need to learn to deal with facts and not be sidetracked by your emotions. If the decisions you make about your future spring solely from your emotions, college professors will not recommend you for graduate school. Think seriously about what I'm saying. Stick with history."

I did not want to be a lightweight, a term he used in history class to describe mediocre reports and term papers, and, in case I got married, I did not want to end up reading vacuous novels to fill empty days, a disturbing picture he deftly etched on my mind to illustrate why housewives were driven to read something other than cookbooks, child-rearing manuals, and ladies' magazines.

I did not question his reasoning or think about rehashing it with my parents. Neither one of them had gone to college so I assumed he knew better than they did what I would face in college. I left his office determined to stick with history and to practice being more levelheaded and reasonable and not let my intuition and emotions influence the decisions I made, but I could not stay away from literature, and not just because it was an educational requirement. His admonition against novel reading left me feeling vaguely guilty until I got involved in the story, and when Miss Graves loosed one of her remarkable insights during class, I knew I wanted to read as deeply into literature as she did, and married or unmarried, I, too, wanted to be occupied in meaningful study.

My second trip to Japan was during the summer of 1961, between my junior and senior year in college. My diary that year was a student spiral notebook. Aunt Elizabeth and Uncle Arthur gave me a round-trip ticket to Japan and tuition for a summer session at a language school in Tokyo as an early graduation gift, and I wanted it more than clothes or a blank check for books.

That summer in Tokyo, I went back and forth on the train to language school and back and forth in my diary between my dissatisfaction with Japanese history and an undeniable yearning to concentrate on literature. My discontent with Japanese history centered on the fact that women and their deeds of obedience and self-sacrifice where confined to a few brief paragraphs within a chapter, within a book, within the required semester's reading list, within all the history textbooks and readings assigned over the past three undergraduate years.

The limitation and restriction of women in history texts brought to mind a picture I had of women confined to the *Yoshiwara*, a pleasure quarter for men during the Tokugawa Period. The houses of pleasure lining the main streets of the quarter were open to men who had the freedom of movement and choice and the necessary money to pay for the use of a woman's body and her studied pretense in entertaining him. The windows of these pleasure houses were covered with vertical bars of wood. Behind these bars, caged as it were, sat beautifully dressed women who, once purchased, were required to provide the buyer an hour or an evening of forgetfulness. The men who could not buy the company and use of a woman's body had to build their dreams around their deeply felt need for a union in which a woman treasured him alone. All of these men had to leave the *Yoshiwara* before the gate was closed for the night, usually around 3:00 a.m.

My gaze stayed on the women who, after the streets were cleared and silenced, and the degree of inner darkness had grown significantly deeper, sat a long while in a deep, hot bath easing the emotional and sometimes physical pain resulting from sex roughed out of a strange man's unsatisfied desire or lust. During their bath, women were left to withdraw within themselves and release their anger and shame in the steam rising from the water. The warm, damp odor of the wooden bathhouse evoked memories of earlier times, before they came to the *Yoshiwara* and discovered more of life's harsh realities.

One woman recalled bathing with her mother when her mother forgot her husband's disappointment in the birth of "a useless girl." The girl remembered sputtering when warm water was poured over her head and her mother smiling at her. If only she could be a child again and make her mother smile.

Another woman confined to the *Yoshiwara* remembered a rainy season in her country village when water flowed in sheets from the thatched roof of their house. She had stolen a few precious, solitary moments to stand on the open, narrow verandah to absorb the rain's energy and inhale the scent of the earth and wet thatch as the water blew over her eight-year-old body.

If her father had seen her invoke pleasure in this way, he would have beaten her. Every pleasantry, every reminder of what might have been made him angry. He raged at their poverty and his helplessness in preventing the slow starvation of his family. The presence of his wife and children were reminders of his inability to provide, and he beat whoever was closest. Her mother beat her, too, though less severely, and the girl suffered quietly through this expression of her mother's helplessness and depression.

Her family had once had to depend on barley to fill their stomachs, but now, there was nothing to eat, and they went out every day to search the fields for plants, roots, or grass overlooked by other hungry villagers. She'd listened when her father discussed her price with a man who came through their village now and then looking for obedient young girls to take back to the *Yoshiwara* to work as maids. The man told her father she would eat rice in the *Yoshiwara*; she couldn't remember the taste of rice. She was sold for the promise of food and the two coins the man placed in her father's hand. Because her family was hungry and needed food, she had not been surprised to see how quickly her father's fingers closed over the money. Yet the sight of the coins in his hand brought on a confusion of anger and shame when she thought her father could have sold her more highly valued brother for a larger price.

Her family had been consumed by thoughts of food, and the girl could not fault their jealousy of the promised meals of rice she was going to eat. Perhaps that was the reason her mother had not come to the door to watch her daughter walk away with the stranger. No doubt her mother had been thinking about the food she would buy with the coins. While it was cooking, she would linger near the bubbling pan to savor its delicious aroma because she knew there would be little food left for her after her ravenous husband and son had satisfied their appetites.

If a woman confined to the *Yoshiwara* lingered too long in the bath remembering her family, she could be overwhelmed with pity for them and resolve once again to rescue them from poverty however great the cost to herself. She had to will her mood to lighten before she left the bath to join the other women in a round of humorous stories and bawdy jokes while they prepared for bed. None of these women denied their bodies were bought and sold every night, but to face it directly, remonstrate with it, rebel against the reality of their existence would bring on the pain of helplessness or an unshakeable depression and possibly recurring thoughts of suicide. A seemingly lighthearted period of humorous stories helped dissipate the despair that had been drawn to the surface by remembering.

Now they were tired and wanted to slip onto the *futons* spread on the floor by the child most recently purchased by the house she was now serving as a maid. The bewildered young girl would eventually realize any claim of parental protection had been sold along with her body. Only sleep or death could release them from confinement within the *Yoshiwara*.

None of the Japanese history textbooks I had read mentioned the tears of humiliation and shame these women washed away with the bathwater. The sacrifice these women made was commended as proof of filial obedience. A young girl was expected to be silent and not protest when she was sold into prostitution. No textbook I had read questioned or raged against the buying and selling of girls and women; it was simply recorded as fact.

At the end of that summer of language study, I wrote these decisions in my diary: (1) to complete my final undergraduate year in Japanese history; (2) to apply for a graduate degree in comparative literature as soon as I returned to campus; (3) to take a seminar in comparative literature with Dr. Smith because she was known among women students to encourage questioning facts stated in textbooks, and (4) to return to Japan for a year before beginning graduate school.

Taking Dr. Smith's seminar that fall ended my long dry spell. Her insightful lectures, common sense and practical advice helped me step out of a confusing bog of self-doubt and learn to trust my instincts again.

From 1962 to 1963, I used another student spiral notebook for my first venture in living independently in Tokyo. Aunt Elizabeth and Uncle Arthur had retired from the military and were living in San Francisco so I was free to live in a university dorm. I determined to take only classes that interested me or design those I wanted, which I was able to do with a private tutor in cultural studies.

The first day of class at International Christian University (ICU), I met Margaret.

"Call me Aggie," she told me. "My family does, and there are ten of us when we're all at home (in Australia)."

Always quick to offer suggestions and never hesitant when it came to questioning proposals under consideration, it was easy to picture Aggie being first on her feet in town meetings. I found much to admire in her fearlessness and determination to live as indigenously as possible, and I loved her offbeat sense of humor that gave our time together a lively, humorous bent.

As soon as we could, we moved out of the dorm into a rooming house for students that looked rundown but was kept quite clean. We each rented a three-mat *tatami* room, approximately six feet by nine feet, because it was the cheapest. Aggie's good humor, sense of adventure, and enthusiasm for things Japanese bolstered my confidence and independence while enlarging the haven we found in those small *tatami* rooms and the working-class neighborhood surrounding us.

We used the public bath in our neighborhood where we could leisurely bathe. The tile tub at the rooming house accommodated the two of us when we had things to talk about, which was most of the time. The problem was the three Japanese male students who also rented rooms did not sign up for a specific time to use the bath as we had been instructed to do by the woman who managed the building, kept it clean, and read the rules to us before we moved in. Just as one or both of us had settled into the deep, hot water for a long soak, one of those impatient, demanding boys would be at the door of the bath to tell us we were a bother and to hurry up.

The following spring after Aggie left Japan to return to Australia, my *tatami* room shrunk to its actual size and the rooming house grew more dismal and depressing without her humor to lighten the hours I had to spend there. I read ads for rooms posted on the school bulletin board and pulled off three that were not farther than five train stops from campus.

When I reached the first house to inquire about the room that had been advertised, the gentle, inquisitive woman who answered the door told me the room had been rented just that morning. She asked what I was studying and how long I planned to stay in Japan before she mentioned the possibility of renting a room with a family who was reluctant to advertise. They were looking for someone who spoke Japanese, a male preferably; nevertheless, since she could understand my spoken Japanese, she thought I should apply. Lady Kindness, I've forgotten her name, telephoned to find out if that family would consider interviewing me, then she wrote the address and directions on a page from my notebook and told me where that neighborhood's police box was located in case I needed further help with directions.

The house was in a neighborhood of expensive new homes surrounded by heavy cinderblock fences and some open ironwork gates. Too modern, I thought, wanting something more traditional and as old-fashioned as the Nakamura's farmhouse. An impatient maid came out to the gate where I was pushing the bell and showed this inept foreigner how to open an unlocked gate and walk up to the door where there was another melodious bell to push if I had any hesitancy about using the Japanese custom of sliding open the door and stepping into the *genkan* or vestibule and announcing my presence.

The maid did not know English or did not trust my spoken Japanese because she used only her hands to direct me into the vestibule where she motioned for me to remove my shoes and to step up onto the hallway and into slippers before she led me to a carpeted room with a piano, overstuffed armchairs, and a prominent liquor

17

cabinet stocked with well-known American and European brands. When she pushed both hands toward the floor as if she were pumping something and pointed to a chair, I understood I was to sit there and wait.

A few minutes later, the well-dressed, middle-aged and thoroughly competent lady of the house entered the room followed by the maid who carried a tray with two cups of strong, excellent coffee. Lady Thoroughly-Competent spoke English very well and did not hesitate to ask direct questions about how I was supporting myself, whether or not I entertained men in my room, what I was studying, and what I hoped to accomplish with these studies, and if my parents had approved this year of study in Japan. I must have passed muster because after we finished our coffee, she called the maid and told her to show me the way to *Obaasan's* (grandmother's) house where I would be interviewed again.

While I was putting on my shoes in the *genkan*, Lady Thoroughly-Competent told me the final decision would be *Obaasan's*. I wondered about that since the earlier stated preference for a male student had probably been Lady Thoroughly-Competent's idea. She was the unmistakable mistress of this large, modern house and possibly the real head of her extended family, as her opinion carried weight, no doubt about it. She asked if she could speak frankly.

"Yes, please do."

"We hope you will profit from your time and study here, and we hope, if *Obaasan* does agree to rent the room to you, you will take her frailty and age into consideration in your dealings with her."

I told her I would act responsibly.

The maid and I did not attempt to talk to each other while we walked the five or ten minutes it took to reach a narrow street of older houses where, much to my joy, most fences hiding these houses from the street were made of gray, weathered bamboo. The maid opened the gate and walked up to the front door. Once inside the gate, I could see *Obaasan's* house was neither new nor large. The maid slid back the door and stepped into the *genkan* and shouted, "*Obaasama!*" No need for a doorbell here.

Stepping into the vestibule, I had the strange feeling I was stepping into a residual well of tradition. There were two large storage jars standing on the *geta bako*, the storage box for shoes worn outside the house. Both jars were streaked with natural glaze, and the lip of the smaller one was chipped. These jars dominated the *genkan* in such a way I was reminded of temple guardians, those larger-than-life human-like figures stationed at the entry gates of temple compounds to prevent evil or malevolent spirits from entering.

Mrs. Matsui came to the *genkan* in response to the maid's loud call and greeted us with quick repetitive bows and a wide smile. She wore a plain brown kimono with a narrow, dark green, vine-patterned *obi* or sash. Her thinning gray hair was pulled into a tight bun at the back of her head. Her upper spine was noticeably rounded by age and osteoporosis. She was no taller than 4'10" or 11". She appeared to be both lively and self-contained, good attributes for a landlady.

We said goodbye to the maid. Mrs. Matsui led me to a good-sized *tatami* room at the back of the house, telling me it was the one available for rent. The only furnishings were a low, Japanese-style table and cushions. The room opened onto a small garden where Mrs. Matsui grew flowers and pots of cucumbers. A fig tree and a small mossy knoll of rocks were proportionately arranged to the right of the garden close to the fence, on the other side of which was a row of narrow houses leading out to another street.

A tea tray had been prepared and covered with a clean towel. We sat on cushions near it, near the narrow verandah that continued past this room around and alongside an old-fashioned kitchen. There was no laundry hanging over the bamboo pole suspended under the roof to block my view of the kitchen's shadowy interior. Farther to the right beyond the kitchen was the bath and toilet, identifiable by the small, narrow window near the top of the outside wall.

Mrs. Matsui bowed her head to the *tatami* in welcome. I bowed my head to the *tatami* in deference to her age. I thanked her when I was upright again for seeing me at an inconvenient time. She brushed this nicety aside and got straight to the business at hand by asking if I had ever used the public bath. It was understood I would want to bathe every day, and her concern was whether or not I would feel comfortable bathing with other women. She told me she preferred going to the public bath because it gave her an opportunity to talk with other women in the neighborhood; consequently, she fired her tub at home only once or twice a week. I told her I had used the public bath during winter months to keep warm, as my room at the apartment house did not have a heater.

It was agreed I would buy my own lunch and dinner and she would provide a simple breakfast with tea in the morning and fill a large thermos with hot water at night so that I might make tea while I studied.

The electricity posed a problem because the room had only one single light bulb hanging in the center of the room. I needed a high-density lamp for study, and during hot, muggy summer months, I wanted to use my electric rotary fan. This additional use of electricity was added to the rent.

She told me where in the neighborhood I could have my clothes laundered, but for a nominal sum to be added to the rent, she would wash my clothes as she now owned an automatic machine, a gift from the big house, and no longer had to wash everything by hand.

She apologized for not having a desk and chair for me to use. These weren't necessary as far as I was concerned because I preferred keeping the room Japanese style. It was agreed I would move in that Sunday when I could hire a small truck to help move my bedding, books, and clothing. On the day I moved in, I would give her an additional month's rent as key money.

After we finished discussing and agreeing on the arrangements, she removed the cloth from the tea tray and placed a cup of tea and a plate of fresh jellied bean paste in front of me on the *tatami*. Ants were crawling over the sweetened food. I crushed them as inconspicuously as possible before taking a cautious bite. Mrs. Matsui chatted on about the house and neighborhood thereby giving the ants time to flee before she took her first bite.

She told me the two rooms on the second floor of her house were used to store boxes of things that belonged to the big house; she went up there only when it was time to clean or a box needed sorting through or moved back to the big house. The *fusuma* or paper-covered doors between my room and the front room where she slept were kept closed. When she opened the outer doors of her front room, she looked out on the narrow, well-tended formal garden that could also be seen and admired by anyone stepping inside the front gate.

I looked forward to the days when I did not have to leave the house for class, when I could stretch out on the *tatami* and read or sit on a cushion before the low table and practice writing characters or read haiku in preparation for an assignment. With the doors of my room slid back for a full view of the garden, my focus was drawn from books into the life out of which haiku springs.

Before she started working in the garden, Mrs. Matsui covered her head with a straw hat and slipped a convenient length of woven ribbon through the sleeves of her kimono in order to tie them back and leave her arms free of encumbrance. She squatted before the hillock of moss, and her bare, brown arm stretched out to pinch a tiny weed and pull it from the ground. She moved that bent arm back and forth, back and forth, placing tiny weeds in a pile near her foot. Wholly concentrated on her task, she reminded me of a large brown grasshopper purposefully designed by its Creator to hunt for a particular leaf or vine.

Her garden could be likened to a haiku, a poem proportioned by a limited number of syllables. The proportions of the garden were limited by the placement of the house on a narrow plot of ground and the surrounding walls. Both the garden and haiku gave me pause. Moments of awareness rose up through my observations to drift away and disappear in currents of warm air and were not recorded in my diary.

Mrs. Matsui's garden and the clear balminess of early spring with longer, sunlit days initiated a season of personal well-being and happiness. I discovered that living alone, in a sense, in a stranger's house was not as lonely as I had thought it was going to be. This was the year I ran into the bookshop to get out of a rainstorm and found the copy of *The Lady Who Loved Insects* in a puddle and brought it home, an unexpected and well-timed coincidence since, as I wrote in the beginning of this diary, that lady's story was just what I needed to return to my first love—literature.

The women I met at the neighborhood bath told me where to find inexpensive sushi and a coffee shop that made delicious iced coffee and French toast, a combination that tasted especially good during those spring and summer months. Whenever I happened to meet a lady of the bath on the street, we exchanged friendly smiles and bows. The lady who kept the fruit and bread store on our street nodded and smiled as I walked to and from the train. She offered light conversation about the weather or seasonal food whenever I stopped in on my way home to buy something to snack on in the evening while I studied.

I ate my evening meal at one of the three neighborhood restaurants offering enough choices, at least for me, of inexpensive traditional Japanese food. Later, during cold weather, if I stayed on after my meal to read and take advantage of heat radiating from a small electric heater placed in the aisle, the proprietor or his wife refilled my teacup whenever they noticed it was empty.

I am counting on these earlier experiences in Japan to support my work on the translation of *Mountain Temple Woman*. I don't know anyone in Kyoto, no women certainly. Professor Hiraizumi would help, I'm sure, in an emergency, yet even without a close friend to talk to, walking around the city will get my responses flowing onto the pages of this diary. I'll call Mom and Dad or Aunt E. whenever loneliness wrestles me to the ground and narrows my outlook.

We left Anchorage hours ago, at least it seems like it. If I don't sleep soon, I will have to wait until I reach Japan.

Wednesday, August 5. I woke when the lights were turned on and a flight attendant announced breakfast. After coffee and while standing in a slow-moving line with other passengers waiting to use the lavatories, a hum of anticipation increased as people talked, stretched, and bent toward the windows and moved into the aisles to put on suit jackets or checked their soft bundles and shopping bags in the overhead bins.

My heart began to race when the clouds parted and I had my first glimpse of Japan from the air. A whole year—a whole year to work in Kyoto!

Once my feet touched the ground at Haneda Airport, I was intent on finding my luggage, clearing customs, and taking in everything that eight years ago had been familiar to me. I stopped in front of a counter with packages of different kinds of *sembei* (rice crackers) for sale. The clerk asked in English if I would like a sample. When I didn't respond, she held out a large, cellophane-wrapped cracker and waved her extended wrist back and forth to help me understand she was offering it to me.

"No charge. No charge," she kept repeating in English.

I stood there unable to speak or lift my hand as I watched the cracker sail back and forth in front of my eyes. I would have become a permanent fixture at Haneda if a group of jabbering, elderly Japanese women had not bumped into me and pushed me aside in their haste to reach the counter where the offer of a free sample waving in the air rallied their ingrained frugality. Thus, I was shaken from my stupor and returned to a normal state of competence.

I had forgotten how crowded it is on this, the largest island of all the islands called Japan. The number of people seated in chairs or standing and walking through the airport boggled my mind. During the past eight years at home, my memory eliminated my aversion to crowds and my aggravation when I am shoved by people who prod me with their elbows and fists or ram the edges of their packages and umbrella handles into my back to push me forward or aside. My memories of Japan have been focused on Mrs. Matsui's secluded garden and the quiet streets of her neighborhood, its steamy, relaxing public bath and the friendly women who bathed there. Even the three-mat *tatami* room where I lived before moving to Mrs. Matsui's house has become more habitable and trouble-free with time. A romantic form of amnesia has airbrushed my memories leaving me with only pleasant encounters to review.

I joined the queue in front of the airport waiting for taxis into the city. When it was my turn, the driver was out of the car in a flash. Just as if he were following the exacting steps of a Kabuki dance, he lifted my heavy suitcase into the air with one hand before drawing his other arm around to place it on the floor of the trunk. I slid into the back seat thinking the short ride into town would be a pleasant interval before boarding a train to Kyoto. Wrong! As soon as we had drawn away from the airport to enter the highway leading into the city, I clung to the seat for dear life as the driver jockeyed for the fast lane and played bumper car and chicken with other daredevils on the road.

The driver must have been guided by some sort of internal radar that measured in centimeters our distance from other speeding cars.

While driving at eighty or ninety miles an hour, he turned around to tell me about the changes that have taken place in Tokyo since the 1964 Olympic Games were held here. His recitation went on and on with only a few pauses, and these pauses were punctuated by a wide smile turned directly toward me in the back seat. I did not hear much of what he said because I thought one of us should be paying attention to the cars swerving dangerously close on either side during our death-defying race into the city.

When we came to an abrupt stop in front of the Tokyo train station, he had my suitcase out of the trunk and on the curb before I could get my trembling legs out of the car. I offered him a tip as a token of my thanks for getting me to the station (alive and in one piece). He refused my offer, saying I was a guest in his country and he was pleased to welcome me again to Tokyo. It was a memorable welcome; my leg muscles hadn't stopped trembling.

My updated impression of Tokyo is a flash of tall buildings, horrendous traffic, the cab driver's wide smile, and taxis that fly on automatic pilot over high-speed roads.

I called the Azuka Foundation today to report my arrival in Kyoto. The representative who had been sent to Haneda to officially welcome me to Japan and to accompany me into the city and to the train station had failed to see anyone with long braids. She apologized. Although my long braids were obvious in the photo they'd requested, I don't remember their mentioning sending someone to meet me when I arrived. I should have anticipated such a considerate detail since my visa now describes me as a visiting scholar and I am no longer viewed as one of the many self-sufficient students passing through the airport.

I apologized to the representative in turn and told her I had slipped my braids into the back of my jacket before I left the plane to avoid having my hair caught in the strap of someone's luggage while we were jostling small bags along the aisle. I did not say I hadn't expected anyone to meet me or that I failed to see a sign with my name on it being held up among others swooping and writhing like a long, jointed paper dragon during a Chinese festival.

Many people consider long braids old-fashioned for someone twenty-eight years old and not employed as a folksinger. College friends and my college students have told me more times than I care to remember that they had worn their hair in braids when they were in elementary school. During my long undergraduate dry spell, I thought about cutting my hair, but it was just an idea I used to turn my thoughts from self-doubt.

My grandmother's crown of silvery white braids and straight posture gave her a regal bearing. After my grandfather died, one of her women friends amazed me when she asked my grandmother why she had cut her hair. Couldn't she see my grandmother was grieving over the loss of my wonderful grandfather with whom she had lived most of her life? Didn't she notice the abrupt downward slope of her shoulders after his funeral? Later, my mother would tell me some people use only their eyes to see.

I wanted a telephone in my apartment this year because I need one to call the States to arrange job interviews and call my parents and Aunt E. Private telephones are expensive here compared to the States. I was told the waiting list for Japanese people is quite long, so it may be something of a miracle that I have one at all. I know only one person in Kyoto to call, Professor Hiraizumi, and he asked me to write to his university address when I arrived. He is on vacation until September.

I just remembered a much earlier experience with telephones. In 1956, there were only two telephones in the Nakamura's village: a red one for public use in front of the drugstore near the village bus stop and a smaller black one in the home of the head or chief villager—kind of like a mayor. Yuriko-san had interpreted the small sign on that family's gatepost as, "This house has a telephone." It was evident that family also had more money and prestige than other villagers. They not only had a telephone, which must have been even harder to get in 1956, they also had a bamboo fence with a roofed gate and wooden doors that slid back easily on metal runners. It was an aesthetically pleasing change from the cinderblock fences surrounding other farmhouses I had an opportunity to see.

The Lady with the Telephone wore the most elaborate hairstyle of all the village women I saw during my visit. Her hair poofed out at the side and was drawn up to rest in an orderly mass pinned on the top of her head, whereas other women I noticed kept their hair short or arranged in a simple bun at the back of their necks. The Lady with the Telephone had a fairer complexion than the other women because she did not have to work in the fields and could avoid long hours in the sun. Mrs. Nakamura and other women who helped with farming chores covered their hair with a towel and shaded their faces with large straw hats whenever they worked outdoors, and still the sun had creased and darkened their exposed skin. The telephone lady's hands were soft and white when she waved me into the room toward the telephone I would use to call Aunt E. to report my safe arrival.

Yuriko-san told me asking to use that telephone was not an imposition, although I felt it as such. She said that family expected other villagers to ask to use it, and someone in the mayor's home would carry phone messages to other villager's homes whenever it was necessary. This kind of generosity and cooperation was expected from anyone in their village who had a convenience that made life easier for all.

My western-style, furnished apartment is on the third floor of a three-storied building. From the wide windows in the dining area and the equally wide windows over the couch, I can look down onto narrow yards that belong to the fenced and gated houses across the quiet, narrow street that separates our tall university-owned apartment building from their low neighborhood of private homes. The street we share travels up between my building and these houses from a wide main street called Higashioji up to the top where it meets another narrow street that branches to the right and left like the top of a capital T. At the top of this street, a tall stone wall separates our neighborhood from Kyoto University campus. The massive stonework reminds me of a fortified castle wall.

Turning left at the top of the T, I can walk out to a wide main street that has several entrances into campus farther up the street. If I decide to bypass the university and continue walking up this wide street, I pass restaurants, coffee shops, stores with local crafts and ceramics, and many other interesting things to consider before I reach the entrance to the Silver Pavilion.

Because my third-floor apartment borders Higashioji Street, I am becoming familiar with street sounds. Higashioji is wide enough to accommodate lanes of traffic and the trolleys that run up and down the middle, yet it doesn't come close to the horrendous proportions Tokyo traffic is apt to reach on most days. If there is such a thing as rush hour here in this northeast section of Kyoto, I have yet to notice or be distracted by the whirr and horns that voice the impatience of drivers. I like hearing the trolley rumbling up the street before it comes to a stop near my apartment building. I find myself smiling whenever I hear its familiar sound.

My apartment's floor plan is a large square, which, at the doorway or entrance, has been divided on the right into a small bathroom with a shower (no tub); next is a small alley-type kitchen and then the bedroom. The bedroom has three walls and windows, of course, and a large white canvas curtain which substitutes for the fourth wall when it is pulled along a rod to separate the bedroom from the living room. Pulling the curtain back and forth reminds me of those scenes from Heian Period scrolls in which rolled-up curtains and the lack of a roof serves to focus the viewer's eyes on the characters and a specific scene.

There is no curtain or wall to separate the dining area and living room that take up the other full half of the square. The sofa is directly beneath the large windows in the living room as this placement takes advantage of the natural light coming into the room. The hard, wooden arms of the sofa needed several pillows before it became a good place to read, sitting up or lying down. The coffee table in front of the sofa holds a scattering of tourist pamphlets, books, and newspapers. One of the two matched armchairs on the other side of the coffee table holds a large box of books between its stiff, wooden arms. Beside it sits its twin with the same hard wooden arms that plead for something to hold, something to hide its lack of comfort and appeal. The sideboard in the dining room stands in front of the large empty wall near the entry door. I'm using it as a temporary bookshelf for some of the books I've unpacked.

I pushed the end of the dining room table up next to the wall under the windows to get the full benefit of natural light. Now I am having second thoughts about using the end closest to the window as my desk because I am too easily drawn from my typewriter into looking at the houses across the street and farther beyond to the tile roofs of other houses that stretch even farther back into quiet, unexplored neighborhoods toward the far distant view of wooded mountains.

In someone's yard not too far away is a tall, stick-like tree with awkwardly angled branches that jut up above smaller, rounded trees. I have yet to see this tall tree bend when strong breezes sway other trees' leafy branches. Its stiff branches remind me of an Adirondack chair, yet birds don't find it unappealing and flock to it at sunset.

The distant view of wooded mountains undulates in a greenish haze above the unchanging line of blue-glazed or dull grayish-black roof tiles in the neighborhood close by. On clear days when I'm out walking, intent on sightseeing, errands, or exercise, I take my fill of wooded mountains wherever the view provides. As long as there are trees, I can manage a year of solitude and study.

I could only imagine these mountains while I was teaching at Southern Women's and working nights in an empty storage closet that once housed an inventory of cleaning supplies. (A sympathetic janitor had helped me locate this hideaway from the freshman dorm and the office I was assigned to share with a cigar-smoking professor.) The storage closet, with its lingering odor of disinfectant and industrial-strength soap, provided the cocoon I needed to get my thesis ready for publication. It offered seclusion and though a narrow window I noted phases of the moon as it passed between branches of one of several live oaks on campus. It was a place to think about what I wanted to accomplish in the years ahead and consider risking a break in my career if I did go to Kyoto. Professor Hiraizumi's encouraging letters and then the Asuka grant gave me confidence about finding a job in the States when I returned.

There were no clouds in the sky the day Southern Women's College officially closed for summer vacation and my first two years of teaching came to an end. I went to the storage closet to collect my typewriter and a shopping bag of papers to prepare for my return flight to California. Warm air floated into the closet through the opened window, and I could hear students laughing in the driveway below and shouting goodbyes, car doors slamming shut, and motors revving up for summer vacation.

As I walked slowly down the three flights of stairs I used to race up nights I could spare from other work, I had no punishing thoughts of regret about not staying in the States and building security into my career. I felt no urge to be more vigorous in shaping my destiny. What was done was done. On the main floor, I pushed open the heavy door of the building, stepped out into the dazzling sunlight, and was momentarily blinded. I felt my skirt float up behind me on a rush of air. I was like a butterfly ready for its first flight, or at least I was ready once again to venture into uncharted space.

How fortunate I am to be in Kyoto at last.

August 7, Friday. On the white, empty pages of this diary, the Lady Who Loves Literature will write about the splendorous days and nights she spends in this, the most beautiful of all tranquil capitals.

I have been exploring the city's museums, temples, and shrines while I play out my urge to see the sights before settling down to work next month. A tourist map is easy to follow. The main streets running north, south, east, and west are broad and not crowded except near the main shopping areas around Sanjo and Shijo where the traffic is heavier, trolley stops are conveniently located, and milling groups of people appear to be spending pleasant hours shopping, eating, and talking about such ordinary things as dress material or a baby who fights sleep. Behind larger stores facing the street, there is a maze of narrow winding alleys with small shops, some almost closet-sized. It took only seconds to decide if these shops offered something I might possibly want when shopping rather than exploring tops my agenda.

I'm expanding my circumference of familiarity with my own neighborhood by taking walks at different times of the day. A midmorning walk took me in and around the residential streets closest to my apartment building. The streets were as clean as I expected them to be and were very quiet, deserted almost. Only one small car was parked near the covered drainage ditch that runs along the street in front of these houses, and the only moving vehicle I saw during this morning's walk was a small, three-wheeled truck.

I met a middle-aged woman wearing a clean smock and carrying a woven plastic basket setting out on a shopping errand. She was curious about why I was walking in her neighborhood and asked, in English, "American?" and "Lost?"

"Yes, I am an American, and no, I am not lost. I live in that apartment building." I pointed to it.

That was enough to satisfy her curiosity, and she told me to please continue enjoying the pleasant weather. We exchanged bows, and she set off again on her errand.

Another woman, startled by the sight of me turning the corner and quickly closing the short distance between us, threw up her arms in surprise, raising the expandable string shopping bag she was carrying over her head as if she were signaling the approach of a foreign and possibly unfriendly plane. The thought made me laugh uncontrollably, and before I could stop and apologize, she had crossed to the other side of the street and was walking rapidly away.

Familiar household smells were drifting out onto the street. There was an appetizing whiff of someone's breakfast soup, *miso*, and farther on, *ramen*, those conveniently packaged dry noodles that can be made into an anytime snack, then the clean fragrance of laundry detergent, a faint drift of incense, and the nostalgic odor, at least for me, of rain-soaked wood that calls up the memory of Mrs. Matsui's wooden bathtub.

When I took the trolley to Gion this afternoon, the conductor called out the names of the stops in such a way the sound of his voice reverberated through my mind like the sonorous sound of a temple bell. The designated trolley stops on the way to Gion offer nothing unusual, nothing I have not seen before when I walked in that direction. Still, his voice stimulated my imagination into expecting the sight of something as magnificent as a vast deer park with wild pheasants, perhaps colorful birds resting on tree branches, perhaps even wild boar moving through tall grass on narrow paths they had previously trampled to dust, or even to be awestruck by the dazzling sight of Amaterasu, Japan's divine ancestor, emerging from her cave with the gift of sunlight to help her people see more clearly into their lives and the work they do, as well as to make the soil productive and stimulate the great variety of life that grows and flourishes on these islands.

We met with nothing as remarkable as a vast tract of open space or anything as fantastical as Amaterasu. At each stop, we lost some passengers and took on new ones before continuing on our way listening to the rhythmic clicking of metal wheels on steel tracks and letting our bodies sway from side to side with the trolley as we traveled along the street. When my stop was called and it was my turn to step down to the street, I left the tram feeling only pleasure in this unique ride.

Monday, August 18. There are no food stores in the immediate area of my apartment building. Near the corner where our residential street opens to meet Higashioji Street, there is a cubbyhole, smaller than the storage closet at SWC, where a patient, elderly woman sits most of the day waiting to sell packets of cigarettes.

Around the corner from the tobacco stand is a store that sells futons, household linens, and those necessary sofa pillows. When the weather gets colder, I will need more than a thin blanket at night. I want to buy a padded quilt, but the fabric on those I have seen in the store is too bright or gaudy. I prefer something more traditional such as Tamba cloth or a *kasuri* pattern from Okinawa. When I asked the proprietor if he would have such a quilt this winter, he sucked air in through his teeth before sighing deeply and turning away to avoid giving me a negative answer.

His inability to say, "Yes (as this is a more positive beginning to a negative answer), yes, I will not have and will not get the quilt cover you prefer," doesn't discourage me. I will stop in every now and then and restate my request. I could look elsewhere, I suppose, possibly in one of the large department stores in town, but our neighborhood futon shop is more convenient and more interesting at the moment than a department store. Who knows? Something may turn up before the fall rainy season initiates a spell of damp, cold weather, and I'm willing to settle for whatever is available.

When I don't want to spend a great deal of time shopping for food, I walk to a supermarket farther up Higashioji Street and not far from the Hyakumanben trolley stop. This store carries a variety of fresh, packaged, canned, and frozen foods, and a European brand of instant coffee with a more robust flavor than its American counterpart. A checkout counter staffed by friendly clerks efficiently concludes the time I want to spend shopping for groceries.

During a late afternoon exploratory walk soon after I came to the city, I discovered a covered alley of dimly lit shops that made me feel as though I had entered a hidden stream of consciousness. The feeling registered as I looked around at other shoppers milling in front of counters with recognizable offerings for sale. I appreciate, as I'm sure other shoppers do, the egg lady's willingness to sell three eggs if that is all that's asked for and the bread lady's willingness to sell just four thickly-sliced pieces of bread to a budget-conscious shopper, and the butcher who efficiently wraps up as little as thirty grams of chicken breast or thinly-sliced beef for stir-frying and thanks the customer for the order.

The man who sells Japanese pickles was prepared to wait however long it took me that day to limit my appetite for *tsukemono* to a modest purchase. He did not fail to keep me in the corner of his eye while he tended to other women who knew exactly which pickle would compliment that evening's meal, and I gazed at open barrels of pickled vegetables, some preserved in sake, to the counter with vacuum-sealed plastic-wrapped packages. I didn't need or want *tsuekmono* for supper that day, but I did buy some to eat at breakfast with rice and tea as this makes me feel very indigenous indeed.

As more women concerned with the evening meal crowded into the aisle, an already lively sense of purpose heightened. The only lights under the tent roof were strings of dim light bulbs, some of which were covered with round dusty paper lanterns, yet poor lighting and a shadowy interior does not hinder the business of buying and selling. Shopkeepers call out the price of meat, fish, or vegetables, whichever they sell, to women with empty baskets on their arms and coin purses in their hands. Merchants are well aware of shoppers who calculate the advantage in saving three yen instead of two. Women shoppers know the limitations of the coins they carry in their purses because they must factor in the necessity of saving for their children's education and the possibility that they or their husbands might linger on past wage-earning status to a very old age.

No one stands still for long, not even the shopper who appears to linger over a small mountain of fruit or a watery barrel of tofu or packages of cookies and sweetened bean paste before deciding what to buy.

I remembered seeing an old photograph taken in China of a candle-lit cave temple where supplicants paused in front of stone-carved Buddhist images recessed in arched and shadowy niches. I saw a similarity in that still photograph and these lively, energetic vendors calling out what they offer to people shopping for the necessary, albeit temporary, satisfaction food provides. These very human Kyoto shopkeepers resembled those stone images in that shopkeepers, too, must spend the majority of their time in the market waiting for customers to buy portions of the necessary foodstuffs they offer.

I was drawn to one vendor whose energetic voice reached out over his counter of ice and fish. In response to his litany of offerings and friendly smile, I chose white fish fillets for my supper instead of the omelet I had originally planned. As I walked home late that afternoon, I mulled over the realization I should not limit my search for understanding to books and temples when markets like this one offer food for thought.

Sunday, September 6. Professor Hiraizumi sent a letter telling me he will meet me tomorrow in his office at the university and someone would phone today to let me know the time. I'm ready. I have exhausted my urge to sightsee and have been catching up on reading. My greater need now is for work.

While I was rereading the professor's article about *Mountain Temple Woman*, I wondered if my level of skill in Japanese will be enough to translate her story from the inside out. If I am incapable of bringing her to life, I will have spent this year formalizing air.

The dreams of success I had while I was in the States do not support me here. Such unreliable buoys are useless anyway. The confidence that bolstered my work in the storage closet has dissolved into doubt. Before I left home, it was easy to imagine myself in Japan bent over dictionaries and my typewriter sailing through the translation. But now, actually living in Kyoto where I need a tourist map to find my way around, my ignorance and lack of experience threaten me with paralysis. I've been afraid to reread the pages I translated at night in the storage closet, afraid they would sound stiff, or even worse, incomprehensible.

I have been walking around this cold, unforgiving apartment on the linoleum-covered concrete floor with my arms wrapped around myself wrestling with the idea my mother was right after all, I should have stayed home and looked for a job in California. Mercifully, after staring for God knows how long at the blur of books and papers scattered on the dining room table, I realize there is no other place for me now but here. Why run from a story that has a life of its own, a life that will integrate itself into mine as my time, effort, and thought are absorbed and used by it. As intimidating as the work appears to be, I want to complete a very good first draft before I leave next year.

A morning spent hugging myself has not been a complete loss because it got me to reread Professor Hiraizumi's journal article several more times and study the picture he chose from several illustrations in the nobleman's diary to illustrate his article. The picture shows an old woman sitting with her legs tucked under her, Japanese style, on the wooden porch of her dwelling, portrayed in this picture as a hut, although it could have been a more substantial building since she came from a well-to-do family and was not poor. It is uncomfortable to sit with the weight of your body pushing your folded legs into a hard surface below, hence the need for *tatami* or cushions. Why didn't the artist show the old woman using a cushion to protect her legs from the wooden porch? It could be he wanted the stillness within her collected position to illustrate her intention of withdrawing from public life, or at least from the official and formal functions that had been required of her while she was living in the city.

The woman moved near the mountain temple in spring. From the porch of her hut, she has a panoramic view of wooded mountains and hills covered with trees with fresh green leaves and pinkish-white cherry blossoms that, in this picture, appear to be haphazardly scattered over the hills like popcorn. Green and flowered hills sweep from the lower left-hand side of the picture up across the mountains to be obscured by her hut before reemerging to push against a cloudless sky and dance off to the right and out of the picture. What a lively view of regeneration this is.

It is reasonable to assume a sense of regeneration would have welled up during her first few days of blossom viewing before it disappeared among other things that would, through necessity, claim her attention. A springtime scene like this one also reminds the viewer of the quiet, hidden work that precedes renewal.

If the woman had been looking at an autumnal or winter landscape, seasons approximated to middle and old age, I might have thought that leaving the city caused her to enter a melancholy or solemn season of her life instead of the brief period of renewal I see in this picture. The lines on her face are carefully drawn. We are not to forget she is elderly. Her clothes are old as well, and faded, although this may be another artistic conceit to underscore the fact of age and the passage of time.

In the distance, a tall pagoda, so tiny in this picture, towers over green trees. The pagoda, a reliquary for sacred objects or remains, is another reminder of the passage of time and the inevitable end of life. Still, it makes sense to assume thoughts about aging and death were kept at bay while she focused on the spring scene in front of her.

Later on, she would be drawn into thinking about the garden she would keep or into watching morning fog lift from the hills or rain pouring from a mass of dark gray clouds passing over the hills, and she would be distracted by the early spring cry of cicadas—the incessant "meeeee meeeee meeeee" people living in Japan get to know. That fall, while peeling the rind from a tangerine, she would wonder if her mortal life would slip away as easily as the skin slipped from this fruit, and while removing the tangerine's inner web of strings, an unforgettable love affair comes to mind. Would her new life in the mountains weaken that affair's hold on her emotions?

She was not a hermit. Several times throughout the year, a garrulous, helpful rice merchant her family had befriended during his youth brought necessary supplies up to her hut. He had much to tell her about city events, his business, neighbors' quarrels and jealousies, his noisy brood of children, and his competent, reliable wife. He related humorous rather than fascinating anecdotes, and he couldn't leave until he told her everything he'd saved to tell her, which meant his recitation could go on long after the moon rose. If she fell asleep during the telling, she woke the next morning to find him asleep on the other side of the low table. After a cup of tea and bowl of hot rice, she listened to the last bits of his narrative before he prepared to leave the mountain.

She would have slipped completely into anonymity if a nobleman whose name she knew from family conversations had not requested time to speak with her. He came to the temple for a specified period of retreat. One of the questions I have yet to answer to my satisfaction is: Why did he want to talk with her? Was it curiosity? Was he seeking diversion from too-familiar rituals and formalities embedded in retreats? Whatever his reason, apparently the timing of his visit coincided with her willingness or need to speak about past events in her life with someone who also sought a meaningful passage. They met frequently during his retreat.

It is interesting to note the nobleman wrote what he'd learned about the woman on the back of sheets of paper on which he had copied out sutras chosen either by the priest or himself to guide his meditation. Paper was handmade, a precious commodity and not wasted. Yet there could be other reasons why he used both sides, and why he used *hiragana,* indigenously Japanese script, instead of the Chinese script favored by the educated class of men to which he belonged.

After the nobleman returned to Kyoto (known to be during the latter part of the Ashikaga Period (1338-1568)), he commissioned a professional painter, possibly an artist-monk from a temple workshop, to illustrate moments of awareness such as the sense of regeneration in the scene of the woman on the porch of her hut. There had been a revival of Sung Dynasty influence and Chinese-style monochrome painting during the Ashikaga Period, yet the paintings in *Mountain Temple Woman* are Japanese in their delicate line drawings and harmonious, faint colors.

The nobleman took extraordinary measures to protect this particular diary. He bound the pictures, story, and sutras in book form and placed it in a secret compartment in the statue of Kannon, the bodhisattva of mercy and compassion, kept in his house. If his family knew about the diary, they did not remove it from the secret compartment when, after the nobleman's death and according to his stated wishes, the statue was given as an offering to the mountain temple where he made his retreat and met the woman. Three hundred years later, when the temple was again being renovated, the diary was discovered. The statue and the original copy of *Mountain Temple Woman* have been kept at the temple and are considered to be two of its finest treasures.

Later: While I was drinking a glass of barley tea and staring out the window at the houses across the street and wondering what Professor Hiraizumi would be like to work with, I remembered another Professor H., Professor Hashimoto, who tutored me in Japanese cultural studies at his home in Ueno. At the time I studied, he had been retired for several years and tutoring only one or two students at a time because his health was frail. A professor at ICU recommended him, and in spite of knowing Professor Hashimoto specialized in the Kamakura Period, I decided to study with him because I could meet with him at his home.

Whenever I stayed a minute past our scheduled one-and-a-half-hour class period, Mrs. Hashimoto, ever watchful over her husband's frail health, came gliding down the hall to slide open the door of his study and offer us cups of lukewarm barley tea. The tea provided an opportunity for casual conversation until I realized I had stayed far too long after class. With apologizes and farewells to both Professor and Mrs. Hashimoto, I left to walk to the train station and continue my conversation with him in my head during the ride home.

Professor Hashimoto was a tall, thin gentleman, who sat and moved through that summer in a graceful, courtly manner that belied how easily hot, humid weather fatigued him. He had been a soldier in north China before the Japanese military bombed Pearl Harbor and America entered the war. While a soldier, he was caught between an instilled Buddhist belief not to kill or harm another being and his loyalty to the emperor. If his commanding officer or any other soldier in his unit discovered he questioned Japan's decision to make war on China, Korea, and Indo-China, he would have been branded a coward or a traitor and possibly shot or hanged. He worried about dying before he could find answers to questions that were making his life as a man and a soldier even more difficult and troublesome.

It made sense to me that a thoughtful man like Professor Hashimoto would return to university to study a period of history when samurai were greatly influenced by the ascetic discipline Zen offered. When he talked about death and Zen-like detachment, I felt he was talking about possibilities he had tasted and chewed on.

The Kamakura Period has too much men's history and too little about women's to suit me; however, as part of the language requirement for that course, I translated two of Professor Hashimoto's articles about the period. Carefully writing out these assignments gave me the idea of translating a Japanese novel someday.

After a class spent listening or talking about how men learned to live and die like ideal samurai, Professor H. closed the period by reading selections from early Japanese poetry. The poems that impressed me most at the time were those written by men in exile. The poet, soldier, or student, in my case, feels the distance separating him from home. In one memorable poem, he locates himself at dusk on the shore of a lake, and in the cry of geese returning to their night's shelter, he hears a reverberation of his own cry of loneliness. I could understand the poet's longing to recover the familiar.

Professor Hashimoto's poetical insight was the reason I asked him to tutor me in Japanese literature, which he did. I had found *The Lady Who Loved Insects* by then and wanted to learn more about it. I listed that short story along with two novels by Tanazaki (*The Makioka Sisters* and *Some Prefer Nettles)* on the course outline we had to submit to the university for approval.

That year, I was living comfortably and mostly trouble-free in Mrs. Matsui's neighborhood. Being a foreigner, I was stared at occasionally while I waited for a train, yet like other people going home from work, school, or shopping, I returned to a Japanese house, a drafty, old-styled house with minimal furnishings and *tatami* flooring; I chose inexpensive food for my supper and usually finished with fruit rather than sweets; I went to the public bath when we didn't fire our bath at home; and I bedded down on a futon and read a Japanese novel in Japanese far into the night.

Later still. Watanabe-san, Professor Hiraizumi's assistant, just called to tell me the time to meet him tomorrow at the main entrance to campus.

That done, I thanked him for delivering the three boxes of books I had mailed to the address Professor Hiraizumi had given me. Although I was not home when they were left at my door, I was pretty sure Watanabe-san had brought them because he sounded young and energetic, a go-getter anxious to please the good professor. We were using Japanese until it was his turn to respond to my thanks for delivering the books. Then he switched to slow, clear English as if to make sure I understood he was "glad to help Professor Hiraizumi" any way he could.

It made me think Watanabe-san was not pleased when being the professor's go-between required working with me. Something like this tells me my self-prescribed, freewheeling tourist jaunts around Kyoto have come to a respectable and timely end. Tomorrow, I become professionally involved with university colleagues, and this requires more thought than I have given to my life as a tourist. I don't want to be clumsy or step on Watanabe-san's sensitive toes, but my size-7 shoes may take up more space than he's willing to share.

I'll wear my favorite one-piece green dress tomorrow and arrange my hair in a crown. First meetings with well-known professors can be iffy, and I don't want to appear as a timid freshman.

Monday, September 7. Watanabe-san and I use English because Sensei (teacher) wants him to practice conversation whenever he has an opportunity.

"Sensei has asked me to help you with resource materials. I've made a copy of the history of the temple where the nobleman spent his retreat. Sensei will give it to you during your meeting with him this morning." Pausing a moment, he added, "I'm speaking frankly when I say those of us who work with Sensei are puzzled as to why he agreed to oversee your translation when he turns down university students who ask him to tutor them in Buddhist art."

"Have you solved the puzzle?"

"Sensei no longer teaches classes at the university. He's resigned from all but two committees. He's handed the majority of his departmental responsibilities to other faculty."

"Is he retiring this winter...sooner?" My immediate concern was whether or not I would have access to his personal collection of materials if he did retire. I was too concerned with how I would manage that to take in what Watanabe-san was telling me indirectly.

"Sensei is ill," he said, clearly impatient with me. "Those of us who work with him know, but he will not tell you because you are a stranger. His illness tires him, and he has to spend time resting at home in order to work at the university. You should not ask for more than he's physically capable of giving."

Revealing this bit of insider knowledge in a straightforward manner appeared to free Watanabe-san from the responsibility of carrying it. He wanted to talk about two other men who were working with Sensei collecting and preparing material for an exhibition of scrolls to be sent to selected European museums next year. Apparently, Fujiwara-san had more to offer Watanabe-san because he figured prominently in the telling, "Fujiwara-san is in Tokyo now with his wife and two adolescent sons. He has been assigned to work here until our part of the preparation for the exhibition is finished. He shares my apartment when he is in town. It's a satisfactory arrangement for both of us because we work all day, and he returns to Tokyo almost every other weekend and whenever else he can. He will be forty-one years old soon. I am thirty-three. How old are you?"

"I am twenty-eight years old."

I assumed we would go directly to Sensei's office, but when he said he had to stop at his office first, I wondered what could be so important it could not wait until after he had taken me to Sensei.

The office Watanabe-san shares with the two other men is not very large to begin with, and it's cramped with their three desks crowded together to make room for a long, narrow table with reproductions of scrolls and other related books and materials spread out for easy access. Akuma-san, the other man in the trio, was sitting at his desk when we walked in. Watanabe-san did not bother to introduce me but walked straight to his desk and stood with his back to me while he shuffled through some papers. Akuma-san did not get up or acknowledge my presence except with a nod of his head after he slipped the "girlie" magazine he had been studying into a drawer. He lit another cigarette and dropped the match into the full ashtray on his desk. He continued to stare at me through clouds of smoke he blew in my direction

Then I understood; Watanabe-san had brought me to their office to give Akuma-san an opportunity to look me over, which he wasn't hesitating to do. He's a predator unable to control his lecherous mind. Any woman could sense it.

I was furious. I told Watanabe-san, "I'll find my way to Sensei's office from here" and stepped out into the hallway ready to walk down every hallway and knock on every door until I found the right office.

Watanabe-san hurriedly joined me in the hall and offered a feeble explanation about how Sensei should be the one to introduce me to members of their group. I didn't buy it. Watanabe-san is young, impressionable, and easily swayed by Akuma (who will no longer get the honorific *san* in this diary). I'll have to stay alert when he's around.

As soon as Sensei and I were introduced, Watanabe-san returned to his office, and Sensei and I sat down to talk briefly about areas of Kyoto I have been exploring while settling into my apartment. Sensei has a distinguished face and thinning white hair. He has clear, penetrating eyes, and his manner is as kind and thoughtful as his letters revealed. The dark blue business suit he was wearing had not been altered to compensate for a recent loss of weight because the jacket hung from his shoulders almost as loose as a cape. If he wore a traditional dark kimono, handsome apparel he could wrap around the full length of his body, his weight loss would be less apparent.

He brought up the subject of his health by telling me it was the reason why our meetings this year would depend on when he is able to come to campus. He didn't name his illness but let his hand rest on his stomach while he talked about his plan to retire next spring, unless, of course, his health requires an earlier date.

Fujiwara-san, who works for the Agency for Cultural Affairs in Tokyo, and whose English Sensei claims is very good because he studied several years in Boston, will act as go-between when he returns to Kyoto, possibly by the end of the month. Fujiwara-san will carry questions about the translation he and I are unable to resolve to Sensei. If I come up against any hurdle before Fujiwara-san arrives, I am to tell Watanabe-san who will then contact Sensei.

Sensei claims Fujiwara-san is knowledgeable about Kyoto's history, art, and architecture; he thinks his intellectual and personal abilities are exceptional. (We'll see. I wonder how he ranks the two other members of his team.) Fujiwara-san, he said, is better qualified than he is to show me areas of the city that will support my work on the translation. (I took this bit to mean Fujiwara-san is in better health and has more stamina than Sensei.)

The good news is that Sensei has arranged for me to use a small office around the corner from his where I can work with materials in his collection, and he took me to that office. It's considerably larger than the storage closet at Southern Women's, but it has two desks. I asked if I would be sharing the room with someone else in the department. I had not seen another woman along the hallway except the office lady who serves tea to men at their desks. I did not want to share a small space with a strange man with whom I would have to be formally polite or someone who might presume that my being a woman, and a foreign one at that, gives him the prerogative of arrogant or immature behavior in his dealings with me. Sensei said I would be the only one using the office, and he gave me the key when we returned to his office.

Sensei was wise to clarify these initial concerns before we went back to his office and sat down on opposite sides of his desk for the more formal part of today's "opening ceremony."

He began, "You must not be discouraged if it takes several more years before you have the experience and understanding that's needed to rightly translate *Mountain Temple Woman*. Unless you are patient and willing to learn, your efforts will result in nothing more than an exercise in the manipulation of language. When it's time to publish your work, you should avoid trying to make yourself more marketable by turning your book into a heavily footnoted academic document.

"Do not strive to be clever or to use your work as a means of advertising yourself. Make your work on the translation your daily practice. If you cannot connect with the deeper qualities within yourself, you are apt to be satisfied with a limited interpretation of the woman's decision to retire from public life. It would be a mistake to view her decision solely as an acceptance of a passionless old age, a way of distancing herself from her youthful affairs."

He also cautioned me against expecting a large readership for my finished translation. He does not think there are many people in America who have more than a passing interest in Buddhism. Americans, like Japanese, he said, are quick to follow the latest trend and to leave it behind as soon as the next widely hyped thing comes along.

It was very quiet in the room at the conclusion of his speech. We sat looking at each other across his desk until I thought to say, "Thank you. I will do my best (meaning, of course, work on the translation)."

He seemed to find this brief response adequate and invited me to tea. When he got up to open the door, I expected him to call the woman I had seen carrying a kettle of tea, but he motioned for me to follow him, and we left campus and walked to a tearoom on a street corner across from campus.

This tearoom has a quiet, pleasant atmosphere, and an adjoining store that sells Japanese-style cakes (something to keep in mind when I need a gift for a special occasion). The shop is decorated with paper shoji and bamboo, and the pottery used to serve tea and cakes is made here in Kyoto. Somewhat incongruous are the waitresses' black uniforms with lace-trimmed white half-aprons and starched white caps trimmed with lace. It's the type of uniform maids wore in 1920-30 Hollywood movies, only never as short as those the tearoom waitresses were wearing.

When the young woman who waited on us greeted Professor Hiraizumi as Sensei, I gathered he must be a frequent patron of the teashop. While the ingredients for our "opening ceremony" tea were being assembled in front of us, Sensei talked about the graded qualities in tea.

"Today, in honor of this day of beginning, we will drink *gyokuro*, the finest grade."

This tea has a lovely green color, a pleasant aroma, and a slight yet noticeable bitter flavor that I liked very much. It was the right choice to begin a year of study and living with traditional values that can sometimes be a bitter pill to swallow.

Wednesday, September 9. Against my better judgment, I went to lunch today with Watanabe and Akuma at the noodle shop they frequent. I took the chair next to the wall across from Watanabe-san fully expecting Akuma to sit next to him, but Akuma wedged himself into my side of the table and pulled his chair close to mine, making me very uncomfortable when he pressed his thigh against mine below the table while he carried on a conversation with Watanabe-san above the table. He must have thought because I wore long braids like some naïve and docile Japanese schoolgirls, I would be silent and let only my trembling lips reveal my consternation when he began rubbing his hand over my thigh.

I turned to him and said, "Warui te (bad hands)." Years before, a female language instructor told me to say this when I complained to her about being groped on the crowded train I had taken to class that morning. She told me this expression would embarrass the person responsible for the groping, and he or she would stop.

I thought I had spoken in a conversational tone until I heard chairs scraping the floor as men at nearby tables moved around to look at us. A flush spread over Watanabe-san's face. I wanted to dump my bowl of hot noodles on Akuma's head; instead, I excused myself to Watanabe-san and left the restaurant. Walking back to campus, my head cleared enough for me to realize Akuma would want revenge for my being an impertinent foreigner and humiliating him in public.

Later, Watanabe-san came by my office to apologize. It was half-hearted at best, but a requirement of his obligation as Sensei's go-between.

Friday, September 11. My nature accommodates solitude and such things as cross-checking dictionaries, comparing texts, library research, and pleasurable hours spent reading related books about history, art, and Buddhism that establish a firm basis and better understanding on which to write my translation; nevertheless, after long periods of close, exacting work, my concentration falters, and the flow of words onto the page slows to a trickle. The best remedy

I've found to restore my ability to concentrate is a walk to the Heian Shrine Garden.

Within the garden, near the entry gate, I sit on a bench and look around at plants and trees. From my place on the bench, my eyes follow the narrow stream that flows toward the back garden wall where it curves around to continue accompanying the path that leads to the now-dormant iris ponds on the other side of the garden. I am drawn into wordlessness; my scattered concentration, my frustration and impatience with my limitations fall away and are left as refuse in the earth. The garden is a good place to bury intellectual and emotional chaos; it holds a promise of renewal that I return to again and again to look for evidence of the fulfillment of that promise.

Usually, walking around the garden readies me to resume work and look for ways to make this long year of solitude work for me. I expect to complete a first draft by next June, but what I would really like to do is finish sooner and leave next spring. And truthfully, although this has nothing to do with work, I would like to meet the man of my dreams, but it's not likely I'll meet him Monday or even Tuesday, so I'm hoping for next year. Here's hoping someone interesting will be working at the same college that hires me.

I left the garden wishing I had at least one companionable colleague here with whom I could talk about life as well as work. My tearoom meetings with Sensei are unfailingly courteous, encouraging, and instructive when I listen for what he doesn't say as well as what he does say. The slow, deliberate way he begins our meetings with tea is a good way to settle in before turning to the translation. I want someone else, someone I can call to tell what I've found in a book or something about a problem or success I've had with the translation, someone I can meet for coffee or dinner to wile away an hour or two with humorous, wide-ranging conversation. I miss laughing with someone.

There's Watanabe and Akuma, both of whom I avoid whenever possible. Watanabe-san recently told me a go-between has been arranging meetings for Akuma and young women also ready to marry. The last two women bowed out, but this, according to Watanabe-san, is not unexpected or a reason to be discouraged. Sooner or later, he says, Akuma will find someone willing to take a chance. I pity that

45

woman. One might have to put up with perverted remarks at work, but no woman wants to live with such a man at home. Akuma's preoccupation with sex is far beyond a normal or healthy interest, as there's nothing funny about the obscene remarks he makes as he slithers by me whenever we chance to pass in the hallway.

Now that I'm engrossed in the translation, I don't go as often to the canvas tent of shops since it's farther from my apartment than the supermarket. Recently, I've found more things to appreciate in this modern market besides speed and efficiency. The women milling along the aisles selecting items for their cupboards at home wear freshly ironed housedresses and aprons. They effuse politeness when this foreigner carelessly steps into their space or bumps the basket they are carrying. If, by chance, they meet another Japanese woman social custom dictates they must acknowledge, their studied, formal politeness as they move around each other with bows, apologies, and smiles reminds me of women I observed at my mother's and grandmother's club meetings and tea parties.

Today, I listened in as two women talked together like proverbial Italians with gestures and big hearts exchanging stories about their children and an outing both remembered with laughter. Listening to those women talking together made me long for casual conversation like theirs to plump up lean, stringent hours I am spending alone. I hoped keeping busy would delay an onset of homesickness at least until Christmas, but I've been ambushed before I was prepared to grapple with it.

I got the homesickness gene from my maternal grandfather. After he graduated from high school and worked with his father building houses, barns, and sheds and tried his hand making furniture, he set out for Washington State because he wanted to see this naturally beautiful place with its magnificent peaks, forested mountains, and coastal islands. He worked in a lumber mill in Clear Lake for over a year until he grew so homesick for Red Oak he had to come home. Shortly after his return, he built our house, married my grandmother, and started a furniture company, designing and building many of the pieces himself.

When I open the door of my apartment and step into the barrenness of these rented rooms and face my reluctance to turn them into some kind of temporary home, I long to run up the steps of our front porch in California and be welcomed by my family.

To the left of our center hall is the living room and also the library with floor-to-ceiling bookcases and cabinets. Tall folding doors separate the library from the living room. While my grandfather was alive, those panels were closed whenever he met with other men who served on school, church, or town boards and committees.

My grandmother and mother, often at different times, entertained their book clubs and members of various organizations in the living room. My mother told me about meetings during World War II when women brought along their sewing and knitting so as not to let up on helping the war effort. She says they were all frightened after reading the February 24, 1942, *Los Angeles Times* report about a Japanese submarine that pumped sixteen shells into tidewater fields at Elwood, twelve miles north of Santa Barbara. The bombs caused only superficial damage to these coastal fields, but that shelling frightened people farther inland and farther north in Red Oak. Women talked about a possible invasion, and my mother's sleep was disturbed by dreams of bombing raids and the possibility war might make me an orphan.

What I like best about our living room at home, besides the wide windows that let in a great deal of natural light, is the long, comfortable sofa with wide padded arms. I read many good books while seated on that sofa. It was the best place to make the book's atmosphere or adventure my very own. After dinner, when my parents or grandparents read aloud, I stretched out on the sofa between my parents or grandparents. It was an ideal place to leave my body while my imagination lived in another time and place.

Across the hall from our living room is the dining room and beyond that is the sunroom, another good place to look up from a book to absorb a fact, an insight, or to wonder at the author's ability to write well-formed, expressive sentences that give shape to vague, incomplete thoughts of my own. I would stare into my grandmother's flower garden seeing only waves of color and sunlight, until dahlias, hollyhocks, California poppies, roses, zinnias, whatever my grandmother was cultivating, came into focus. When I could see flowers clearly again, it was time to return to the book in my lap.

One evening, when I walked past the dining room on my way to the kitchen to get a glass of water, I was enveloped by the scent of roses drifting through the sunroom's open windows and into the dining room and hallway. The air was permeated with that lovely, unmistakable fragrance, and I was held captive by the scent until my father came down the stairs and asked why I was standing in the dark. I associate roses with my grandmother and my grandmother with roses although she grew a variety of other flowers as well.

There are four large bedrooms on the second floor of our house plus a smaller one at the back that looks out on the vegetable garden my grandfather and father planted every year. The small bedroom has undergone many transformations. After my grandparents married, the room was used by the hired girl who moved in and earned her board and keep and a small wage by helping my grandmother get started with housekeeping. The girl had left her family's farm because she wanted more time to study and prepare for college. She stayed with my grandparents for over a year until her aunt took her to San Francisco where she eventually graduated from college and became a teacher.

That back bedroom took on greater importance the year my father moved into our house when he was seventeen. Then, after my parents married and my father joined my mother in her large bedroom, the small bedroom became a sewing room. Before I entered high school, it was redecorated again when I decided to move into it because I wanted to look out at the vegetable garden while I did my homework.

My father was thirteen when he first came to ask my grandfather about working in the garden after school. My father's father had recently died, and his two older brothers had left Red Oak for Los Angeles or thereabouts to look for work by which they could support their mother and three younger siblings. My father had to contribute as well, and he asked for work he could do after school and on weekends.

My grandfather found much to like in young Julian O'Brien, whose blue eyes, dark, wavy hair, and quiet, sensitive nature had already made a favorable impression on my mother. They were in the same class at school. They played games at recess and competed against each other in spelling bees and geography quizzes. They made taffy and bobbed for apples at parties my grandparents gave for my mother and Aunt Elizabeth and their friends, and they ice-skated at the town rink. Almost four years later, when my father's two older brothers returned to Red Oak to move the family to southern California, my father moved into the small back bedroom.

Grandmother O'Brien had dedicated my father, her third son, to God, and she determined he would become a priest. She planned to send him to a Jesuit College and seminary after he graduated from high school. While a young boy, Julian thought a life of quiet study and caring for a monastery garden would suit him, but he was too young to know his emotions would change as he grew up into adolescence. His mother, however, continued to mistake Julian's quiet, serious, non-confrontational nature as agreement with her fixed plan for his life. She failed to notice how his heart and focus changed in his early teens when he knew he loved my mother.

When his older brothers came back to Red Oak to move the family to Los Angeles or thereabouts, my father told his mother and brothers he did not want to leave Red Oak. He did not want to become a priest; he wanted to marry my mother someday. Grandmother O'Brien dispatched her eldest son to have a talk with my grandfather, in the library and behind closed doors. The upshot was, before Grandmother O'Brien left Red Oak, she disowned Julian, saying my Presbyterian mother had bewitched him into leaving the Roman Catholic Church. She told him she no longer counted him as one of her sons and made her four other children swear on the Bible they would have no further contact with him.

(My father once hoped he could reconcile with his family and tried to contact them after they'd moved to Los Angeles. His letters were stamped REFUSED and returned by the post office. Many years later, the letter containing the announcement of my birth was also REFUSED and returned. When Grandmother O'Brien died, someone sent my father her obituary notice. In that brief biography, my father was not named as one of her sons, and I was not named as one of her granddaughters.)

My grandfather took my father in and counseled him to not speak of marriage to my mother until after they had graduated from high school and my father had been working steadily at a job for at least a year. My father took a job with the post office in Red Oak. He got to know most of the families on his mail route by talking with women who were home and waiting to receive their mail and by learning the names of children who called to him from a porch or yard. During World War II, while he was an air raid warden, he walked through familiar neighborhoods where parents and children called to him from porches or opened doors.

My grandparents lost their first two children in a diphtheria epidemic. Their four- and five-year-old boys died just a few hours after they'd been diagnosed. My grandmother was pregnant at the time with my mother, and the doctor and my grandfather kept her out of the sickroom as a precaution. For a long time after that, my grandmother thought if she'd been allowed to care for her sons, they would have survived. It was no help at the time to know other parents in Red Oak had been unable to prevent their children's deaths from this contagious disease. The epidemic took five young lives and mobilized the community to draw up plans for a local hospital.

My mother told me when she learned she was pregnant after nineteen years of marriage, the unexpected, joyful news dislodged my grandmother's guilt about the deaths of her sons. Yet, who can say with any certainty if such news really did extract the guilt? I didn't know my grandmother well enough as a woman to venture such a guess.

I see my grandmother from two angles: From the side, I see a tall, regal-looking woman with fine skin, a perfect profile, a crown of white braids, small emerald and diamond earrings screwed to her tiny earlobes, and a matching pendant on a silver chain catching light as the movement of her breath pushed the necklace forward into the light. It is from this side angle I know her as the stately woman who prompted me in habits of posture and good behavior, who taught me how to embroider, how to sit quietly and patiently at tea parties and to speak politely or not at all to the women who made me uncomfortable when they called attention to my dark eyes or thick hair and the long braids I was determined to grow.

The other angle is a full view of my grandmother's face and the wide, welcoming smile she turned toward my childish enthusiasm for leaping up into her open arms to hug her neck and be hugged in return. When she bent her knees to prepare herself for the impact of my leap, her flowered apron spread across her dress to receive me. Flowers bloomed everywhere around my grandmother—on her clothes and in the scent she wore, as well as in the garden. Her dedication to gardening and especially the scent of roses have left an indelible impression of a woman who worked out her grief and other personal problems while cultivating colorful, fragrant flowers for all of us to appreciate and enjoy.

The third floor of our house in Red Oak is an attic and must remain so in order to accommodate the great amount of family history stored there. A great many different-sized boxes, trunks, and pieces of furniture fill that large room because my grandmother was never quick to throw anything away she thought our family, a relative, or close friend might find useful later on.

The attic windows let in slanting columns of dusty light that left rectangular spotlights on tiers of boxes and the floor. When I was little, I liked to stand in a spot of dusty sunlight and wait for the harmonious blending of my mother's and grandmother's ooooh's and aaaah's and "remember this" that followed the rustling of tissue paper. To me, these expressions were a song that accompanied a special object's resurrection and relocation in contemporary time and space.

I was curious about the dead boys' clothing my grandmother had packed in a special box and stored in the attic, but I could never bring myself to ask her to show me their clothes. I don't think of these boys as uncles because they are always children in photograph albums and family stories. They are too young and too distant to measure up to my very real, knowable, heroic, and special Uncle Arthur. Besides, the deaths of my grandparents were my personal introduction to grief, and it's what my parents, Aunt E., and I have to deal with.

The attic was also the place where my colonial ancestors lived, or so I imagined when I was a child. Their children came down the attic stairwell while we were asleep to play in the hallway and on the stairs, taking turns sliding down the two banister railings separated midway at the landing by a railing wide enough for a child to sit on to test her balance. Sometimes, the ball they played with in the hallway rolled into my bedroom, and my cousins, or so I thought of them, had to float through my door to retrieve it. By the time I'd been born, there were no young cousins for me to play with. If I couldn't have a brother or sister, I wanted a girl cousin my age to come to family picnics, eat Thanksgiving and Christmas dinner with us, play games, and read books with me and pick cucumbers and fresh peas for our dinner.

In my dreams, my older ancestors, and they were always elderly, marveled at the sheer fabric of the new curtains my mother had hung in the living room, not at all like the unbleached muslin they hung at windows in their cabins, if they had unbleached muslin to hang. One of them remembered hearing about China when he was a boy and wondered if the curtains were made of silk. (They were rayon, a popular fabric, my mother tells me, after World War II.) Aunts floated into the kitchen attracted by the aroma of the apple pie we'd had for supper. They admired the new gas range yet wondered how we'd cook with it when they couldn't locate a box for kindling. When one ancestor saw the great number and variety of dishes in the cupboard, her lips tightened censoriously, looking very much like my idea of embittered Grandmother O'Brien, when she told the others, "One set of dishes would do. It's vain and extravagant to show off wealth."

I liked stories my mother told me about our ancestors who left England sometime around 1670 to come to North America. A partial history of our early family was kept in a special cabinet of photograph albums and other family memorabilia in our upstairs hallway near the door leading up to the attic. My mother has told me I'd cling to her dress when she took that ribbon-wrapped packet out of the drawer and unfolded the dry yellowed sheets of paper to show me the graceful handwriting. I must have expected my ancestors, like the paper dolls I played with, to unfold from those sheets of paper and line up on the cabinet in their drab linen clothing to be inspected.

In kindergarten and elementary school, whenever we sang about amber waves of grain and purple mountain majesties above the fruited plains, I imagined my ancestors walking through those waves of grain as they crossed the vastness of North America to reach Red Oak. My grandfather attempted to correct this imaginary picture by telling me farmers would not like people trampling through their fields of ripe grain, but with every singing of the national anthem, my ancestors would again trample through fields of grain. After all, they had to get to California and Red Oak where I was born. Growing up with a truncated record of my ancestors and their vague presence in our attic and my dreams, as well as numerous library books about colonial life in America and stories about settlers migrating across the plains, all became part of what motivated me while still quite young to want to study American history.

The first field trip Red Oak Elementary School students took was a walk to gather leaves scattered on the ground under the Northern Red Oak for which our town was named. In school, we learned to distinguish Northern Red Oak leaves from scarlet oak, as well as the names of a variety of oaks belonging to the *Quercus* (beautiful) family of trees widely distributed throughout North America and other parts of the world. The Northern Red Oak had been in the town park when it was just a cow pasture, along with two other oak trees that were split by lightning in thunderstorms decades apart. My grandfather told me, "Only God knows why this tree weathered damaging storms throughout the intervening years and the two others didn't." While he was working at the lumber mill in Washington, my great-grandfather had written him a letter in which he described the golden-red color of the leaves that particular autumn.

Writing about Red Oak today makes me realize I have brought more of Red Oak with me to Japan than I could have imagined while I was packing to come here and deciding what to bring to add homey comfort to temporary quarters. I brought the bed linens and dresser scarf I embroidered with my grandmother, but these items are no inoculation against homesickness, and working everyday on the translation is not consuming all my time and thought as I hoped it would. Still, writing about Red Oak as I have been doing restores my willingness to live through whatever homesickness comes my way. Homesickness is a temporary condition. I will stay the year and complete a very good translation.

Wednesday, September 16. Occasionally I vary my routine of study, exercise, more study with an early-morning walk to the Hyakumanben trolley stop where I turn left onto a narrow street that winds through a quiet neighborhood until I reach the Kamo River. If I am fortunate, the timing of my walk coincides with a shopkeeper pulling up the corrugated metal shutter that protects his merchandise from thieves during the night. He busies himself with the task of moving boxes of bright, ripe produce closer to the street, a colorful way to attract customers.

As I walk along the residential street of houses secluded behind fences, I may have to skirt around the woman scattering water on the dry, dusty street in front of her gate. We exchange smiles and bows and possibly a comment or two about the morning's weather and the general promise of the day.

Farther on, I notice the woman whose turn it is to be caretaker of a small shrine built into the corner of a narrow, walled lane that leads away from the wide street back to her more secluded neighborhood. It takes her just a few minutes to complete a ritual cleansing of the shrine with water, replace the wilted flowers with fresh ones, and light a stick of incense before stepping back to face the refreshed shrine and respectfully clap her hands and bow before walking back down the lane to her house. She's probably heard many times how this small task contributes to her neighborhood's well-being. My chance observation of the care and attention given to the shrine had me considering its strategic location at the corner I pass when I walk in this direction.

In the cluster of shops near Demachi-Yanagi train station, just before the bridge, a middle-aged woman with an exceptionally lovely face sells paper products, laundry detergents, bath soaps, and other household necessities. She usually disappears through the doorway at the back of the store when she sees me walking toward her shop. Once, in August, during my earliest explorations of the city, I came upon her inside the store while she was gaily moving about, wholly absorbed in slapping boxes of detergent with a feather duster. Sensing someone behind her, she turned around, saw me standing on the threshold, and fled through the door into the family's living quarters. Her daughter came out to wait on me.

That day, I did not need detergent or aluminum foil. I was intent on integrating previous experiences in Japan with my pleasure in exploring this ancient and modern city. Looking into her shop, I saw stacks of flat, gray sheets of toilet paper, the kind both the Nakamura's and Mrs. Matsui used when I lived with them. The discovery had me feeling like an archaeologist who unearths a key artifact that helps her understand more about the lives of an ancient, cultured people—a special moment, indeed. I carried that stack of toilet paper back to my apartment, swinging it at times by my side like a folded umbrella, yet not so self-absorbed I failed to notice smiles on several faces turned in my direction.

Today, on my way to the river, the woman was standing near the front of the store stacking the more familiar rolls of white toilet paper. The reflection of the morning sun on her white smock and stacks of white bathroom tissue made her beatific face luminous. I bowed my head to the Lady of Paper Products and Household Cleansers. She returned my bow and did not flee, holding her ground as I walked by. Perhaps she could tell by my steady pace I had no intention of stopping to buy a necessary item.

If the weather is right, I stop on the bridge to watch early-morning mist suspended above the river, especially if the mist rises in ghostly stalks of rice. Once while I was standing there, I caught sight of one of the bearded men who live in cardboard shelters under the several bridges spanning the river as it flows through the city. That day, a bearded man was walking alongside the river, away from his paper house toward the mountains that are far beyond the bridge on which I was standing. The practice of these men must be to abandon their dwellings early in the day because whenever I have made a wide arch from my apartment to walk alongside the river, their makeshift quarters appear to be deserted. They may be required to leave during the day if local authorities consider their lifestyle a vagrancy they do not want townspeople or visitors to notice.

On bright sunlit days, the Kamo River sparkles and appears to be cleansed of debris that is noticeable on closer inspection. The river is a magnet that pulls people to its banks as it flows through the city. Along its sides, individuals and small groups of human beings grow like plants with heads that bob up and down as they look from the sparkling water to the blue sky overhead and then back again to the river.

If I have time, one of my favorite spots from which to watch the river is a bench across the street from the Demachi-Yanagi train station close to the sandy point where two branches of the river meet. Here, children put dry wood to sail on the current and make contests of throwing or skipping rocks out toward the middle of the river. On warm, clear nights, parents and children return to this sandy point to light fireworks that open like silvery pom-poms against the darkened sky.

On my way across the bridge today to spend time writing letters in one of my favorite coffee shops, I stopped to look down into a calamitous rush of water. The river was swollen after recent heavy rains, and its muddy brown water was churning furiously in its earthen cradle. When I could pull myself away from its hypnotic force, I was struck by how white the knuckles of my hands had become while I was holding onto the bridge railing.

Thursday, September 17. My work is going well. Getting up in the morning and going to my office on campus has its own predictable and pleasurable rhythm. My nights at home can be productive and short when I spend them with histories of Buddhism, religious texts, and books about temple art and architecture.

I've also had mornings when I go directly from bed to the books and papers I left on the dining room table the night before. Nothing intrudes to hinder the revision of yesterday's work, and it's easy to find the right words to shape and color my translation. Uncommon mornings like these are especially gratifying.

There are times in my office when I get worked up about how to translate a particular word or rewrite a sentence. If I stand up and move around in the narrow space between the two desks, sometimes the reward is the word I need, or one that works for the time being. If limited pacing brings no relief, I leave the office and walk to the Silver Pavilion, not far from campus. Once inside, I slow to a snail's pace as I follow the path within this fifteenth-century retreat that eventually opens to a view of trees and shrubs growing up toward the mountains. The peace and silence surrounding those distant peaks slips down to these lovely foothills where it is absorbed by the nearby trees and shrubs, the pavilion, and me.

Monday, September 21. Today brought a needed variation in my usual work-exercise-work routine. I woke up this morning knowing I'd made the right decision about coming here, although, as reaffirming as that is, it doesn't let me forget my need to find a job in the States next year.

I stayed in bed thinking about how work on the translation has taken over my waking life: how words and sentences I've translated do not stick to the pages I've left on the dining room table when I leave to go for a walk, but cling to my mind where they limit my awareness of everything around me except the direction I've taken. If I stop to buy fruit, words I'm holding onto slip into a crevasse in my brain while I talk with the bread lady about the qualities in fresh or dried persimmons. Or if I see a driver impatiently tapping his steering wheel at the corner of the busy street I want to cross, imminent danger drives these words and phrases into waiting pools where they mingle with nascent thoughts until my feet safely touch the opposite curb, then they rush back in newly formed sentences and clear ideas about what I labored to find while working at home. Subtleties and nuances that escaped me in my apartment do not wait outside the door of the restaurant where I decide to have an early dinner. Words hop on the *hashi* I use to transport rice or noodles to my mouth and form coherent phrases I write in the notebook I now carry everywhere to preserve these sparks for later review.

Staying in bed was no longer pleasant when rapidly changing thoughts began to flit around in my brain like a field of fireflies on a warm June night. Getting up and taking a shower was a good way to shake them off. The warm water was perfection, running over my upheld arm in narrow rivulets and then down my back until a skirt of water covered my buttocks. It took only a few minutes in the shower to make room for this memory of shared baths:

While I was living in Mrs. Matsui's house, I preferred going to the neighborhood bath later in the evening after mothers with young children had left to put their relaxed, sleepy children to bed. Around the same time the younger women were leaving, several older women came to bathe. These Ladies of the Bath gathered in one corner of the communal tub to soak in hot water and talk about this or that. Mrs. Matsui disparagingly named three of these women "the committee" because they were obviously overbearing and intent on having their way as well as being responsible for assigning various tasks for the upkeep of the neighborhood to individual households. Except for the obligatory exchange of polite greetings, Mrs. Matsui ignored them by choosing to go to the bath with a friend at whatever time of day that woman was free from caring for her husband who had been crippled in a work accident.

Before I got to know individual ladies by name, I thought it strange that two who shared a bawdy sense of humor guffawed whenever they talked about the recent occurrence of earthquakes in our neighborhood. Either I had slept through these tremors or I had been in Ueno studying with Professor Hashimoto. I wondered how to prepare myself to meet a catastrophe and started by asking what time of day these earthquakes had occurred.

They answered with an outburst of hearty laughter that sent waves across the tub. I was puzzled as to why these women thought earthquakes were a source of humor until one stopped laughing long enough to tell me they had been alluding to the daily *marrying*, as she politely named it, of the newlyweds who had recently moved into the neighborhood.

I became aware of this young woman one afternoon when I stopped to buy fruit and snacks and overheard her tell the bread lady about her recent marriage and moving into the house that touched Mrs. Matsui's garden wall at end of the narrow alley of connected houses. Her demeanor was shy and modest. The bawdy women thought the luxuriant growth of her pubic hair was an unmistakable sign her passion caused the earth to tremble.

I liked to be at the bath when Mrs. Takahashi was there because she told stories as if she had just heard them from a knowledgeable visitor from old *Edo* (an earlier name for Tokyo) or Kamakura. Her anecdotes were more like folktales that centered on a mysteriously insightful or religiously significant happening in the life of a historically well-known noble or shogun.

The happenings she reported were inconsequential and unsubstantiated as far as history books are concerned, but they are of interest to ordinary people like me in that Mrs. Takahashi's stories revealed deeper qualities in the man who occupied a position of enormous power, a human being like the rest of us who through unforeseen circumstances comes to acknowledge a heretofore unknown aspect of his character. If Mrs. Takahashi's anecdote revealed the man's judicious or kindly qualities, this was what I took with me to supper on my way home and what I would later stare at in the dark after I had gone to bed.

Mrs. Nagashima, another Lady of the Bath, was the most reticent and self-effacing of all the Ladies of the Bath. While all of us were soaking in the hot water, she distanced herself from everyone by using overly polite women's language. I came to see her use of this form of polite speech as a linguistic purdah, a barrier or shield she built to hide behind in order to withstand the "Committee's" trampling on her natural reserve and their obvious intention of silencing altogether her soft-spoken interjections.

When she and I happened to meet on the street, she wasted little time with exquisite phrasing. Anguishing over our mutual need to understand each other's country and culture, she encouraged me to attend flower shows and art exhibitions at one of the city's large department stores. She pressed notices of events she had cut from an English-language newspaper into my hand, making noises and gestures that reminded me of a mother bird intent on teaching a baby chick to fly.

The day after we'd had an interesting group discussion in the bath about various kinds of Japanese pickles, Mrs. Nagashima waited for me near the bread lady's store for my return from school. She wanted to give me a boxed arrangement of rice and vegetables she had prepared for my evening meal along with fresh cucumber pickles she had made that morning. (I had said these were one of my favorites.)

Then in November, after we heard President Kennedy had been assassinated, Mrs. Nagashima came to Mrs. Matsui's house to express her sorrow over the president's tragic death. Correctly sensing I would not want to go out to a restaurant for dinner, she had brought a bowl of *oyaku domburi*, rice with egg and chicken, a favorite of mine.

Every night for a week after the assassination, Mrs. Matsui fired her bath at home. Long private soaks in deep hot water provided a place for me to withdraw into empty, blank moments or give in to tears and a longing for home. During that first week, when the news stunned with each telling, Mrs. Matsui opened the sliding doors between our rooms and invited me to watch the evening news on her television. Reports of the assassination were repeated to redundancy, and still we watched. When the funeral procession passed by on the screen in a slow expression of sorrow, I grieved for more than the loss of the president.

When I returned to the public bath after the tragedy, the Ladies of the Bath averted their eyes and made room for me in an area of the communal tub as if that very spot had been designated for someone suffering from shock and sorrow.

On December 8, Pearl Harbor Day in Japan, the remembered tragedy of the Second World War brought tears to Mrs. Nagashima's eyes while we stood talking on the street, although any remembered tragedy or misunderstanding could serve as a release for her pent-up emotions. She would seek me out on the street when anguish built up to the point where she needed someone to listen until she could be delivered from these troubling emotions.

The quickest way to allow her distress to move beyond its moored position was to nod my head now and then to signify I was listening to what she said. Before I realized this was the response she wanted, I thought sympathetic, consoling words would dilute her anguish. Casting unnecessary words into the flow hindered movement of her troubled feelings, and it could take another five or ten minutes after I'd inadvertently stepped into the flow of feeling before she could speed her agitation along to some quiet, containing pool, and we could, at last, say goodbye.

The Ladies of the Bath were well aware of her habit of latching onto a newcomer. They knew when the new bride in the neighborhood grew tired of Mrs. Nagashima's emotional outpourings, she would rejoin the Ladies of the Bath, adding another number to the group that limited Mrs. Nagashima's participation. Mrs. Nagashima, in turn, would retreat once again behind her barrier of formally polite language to signify her acquiescence to the Ladies of the Bath and her release of the new bride back to the group.

Much later. After breakfast and before opening a book, I walked to the Handicraft Center to buy woodblock prints I could no longer live without. As I walked, I thought that for a person like myself who grew up with a kinship to trees and mountains, Kyoto's setting among wooded mountains, open sky, gardens, temples, ancient architecture, museums, rivers, a low skyline for the most part, a slower pace of life, a moist climate, and those wonderful trolleys, was perfectly suited to my nature.

I bought two affordable reproductions of Hiroshige's prints that I have wanted for some time. My favorite, *Squall at Ohashi*, is one of his *One Hundred Views of Famous Places in Edo*. It shows several people crossing a bridge in a downpour. Three travelers lean their bodies into the storm as they walk across the bridge toward the side of the river where grayish silhouettes of houses and other buildings await with the promise of shelter and, I would hope, cups of hot tea. I feel the wonder and wetness of rain in this print.

The other print, *Geese Alighting at Haneda*, is from Hiroshige's *Eight Views of the Edo Environs*. In this print, tiny pilgrims wearing wide round hats are dressed in white robes caught by a breeze as they leave the shrine to head toward that evening's shelter. Geese flying in formation across the sky are also heading toward a night's rest among the reeds. Professor Hashimoto had this print in his study, and I've connected it to the evocative poetry of exiles he read at the end of our class. It's a sentimental choice that suits my mood when I'm feeling the distance from Red Oak. Walking home on a Kyoto street at sundown and smelling onions frying in a householder's wok in preparation for the evening meal can make me ache with longing for home.

I stopped in another gallery to buy a contemporary print with a line of six red-bibbed stone *jizos* under a narrow roof that offered some protection from the eroding effects of rain. The roof is too dark to distinguish detail clearly, but I imagine patches of moss growing there because it's a given in this humid climate. In front of these *jizos* is a tall, gnarled pine tree with roots jutting out of the ground as if to confirm the evergreen's life both above and below ground.

I have a *jizo* about twelve inches tall at home in Red Oak which I bought because I liked the coarse, gray stone out of which this figure of a compassionate bodhisattva was carved. The Red Oak *jizo* has a round, shaven head, just like his six cousins in the print I bought today. *Jizos* are considered to be favorably disposed toward travelers, children, and pregnant women. They are often seen in shrines at crossroads, for who hasn't been, or will be at one time or another, at a decisive crossroad in their life? I have seen more elaborate and exquisitely carved *jizos* in museums and photographs that cause me to marvel at the craftsman's skill. Still, I find the simple columns of stone I've brought home more approachable.

When I did come home to hang these prints and look around my apartment to see what else would make it homey, I decided to spend the rest of the afternoon looking through pottery and bamboo handicraft stores on the street leading to the Silver Pavilion. I had promised myself I would look more carefully when I had time. Well, today I had time.

I found several small things to buy for friends at home and a cherry bark vase I could use on the sideboard in my dining room.

A rejuvenated interest in the world beyond books gave me an appetite for food as well as art. I had wanted to try the corner coffee shop near a bridge passing over a stone-lined gully. The coffee shop has large windows facing both streets, and from where I was standing on the street, I could see it was empty. It was almost two o'clock; people with jobs had returned to work, and women walking on the street would not be ready for coffee so soon after their noon meal.

All I could see of the single customer sitting in the back of the restaurant talking to a waitress was his legs. I took a table near the door where I had a wide view of passersby on the street leading to the Silver Pavilion. I ordered a sandwich and a cup of coffee from an attractive young waitress and turned back to the window pleased with how my break from work was a pleasant change.

I turned as someone approached from behind. It was Watanabe-san carrying a cup of coffee.

"May I join you?"

"Yes, of course."

"You aren't working at the office today?"

"No, household errands have consumed my time. You're taking a coffee break?"

"Yes, a coffee break. I am taking a coffee break. Will I see you at the office tomorrow?"

"Most likely."

Watanabe-san must think I don't remember how good his English is when he wants to play pattern-drills we both learned in language study. He is determined to ferret out information about my personal life, so much so his questioning borders on interrogation.

The first day we met, he'd asked my parents' ages.

I told him they were 104 and 105 years old.

Then he asked, "How much money did you earn while you were teaching in America?"

"I earned one million dollars each year I taught in America."

He had laughed at this, and our conversation turned to things he wanted me to know about Sensei's health.

Watanabe-san pretends he doesn't understand he's being rude when he asks personal questions, but we both know it's a screen he hides behind to see if I will satisfy his curiosity. He has many misconceptions about Americans, especially women, and tries to see what he can get away with before his own sense of decency and self-respect catches up and calls him on being rude. The purpose of these language drills is usually to ferret out my sexual experience.

Today, the question was, "How often do American women have sex?"

To end it before it began, I told him, "Literature is my field of study, not physiology. Dooo youuuu un...der...stand?" I drew the words out as if he could understand only the simplest English.

"Yes, I un...der...stand." He laughed.

We both laughed, and my irritation dissolved. He does have a sense of humor.

Being interrogated about my private life has not been my only beef with Watanabe-san. Early on, he thought he had the right to exhibit me to other men curious about foreign women. After taking me to his office that first day to be stared at by Akuma, he then brought two men to my office where they crowded in hoping to have their curiosity satisfied. I had no chance to stand up unless I could get behind my chair with my back against the wall, which I couldn't without touching one of the three men standing over me. Watanabe-san didn't bother with introductions, probably because one doesn't when viewing a monkey in the zoo.

He expected me to sit quietly in my chair while these two men stared and gaped at me in between nervous laughter they shared with each other. Since they didn't poke or jab me with sticks or throw peanuts I would be expected to grab and eat, I did sit quietly, saying nothing, but inwardly, I was fuming. I fumed the rest of the afternoon, or whenever I thought about it, but by the end of the day, I could excuse Watanabe-san's thoughtless behavior because he is helpful whenever I question him about materials in Sensei's collection, and he has a sense of humor we're beginning to share. Besides, he's likeable.

The very next day after he led that disastrous tour of the two strange men, he brought another man to my office. This eager stranger introduced himself in English, telling me he worked in another department and, not wanting to offend a foreign guest, tried to engage me in conversation. I stood up and interrupted him saying I was much too busy to talk as I had a great deal of work to complete. Both men stepped back into the hall, probably expecting me to throw a chair after them. As I was leaning on the door locking it, I heard the stranger say, "The foreign woman is rude!"

Watanabe-san is used to the Japanese custom of sliding open vestibule doors and announcing his arrival. My unlocked office door made it too easy for him to interrupt whenever he thought of something else related to his assignment as go-between. Now, I keep the door locked. When he does come to my office, I wait until he knocks lightly on the door and says his name, even though I can distinguish his shadow through a frosted-glass panel. Then I stand in the open doorway trying to fill it up with the stern, forbidding presence of a schoolteacher while he tells me the date and time Sensei wants to meet me at the tearoom or both of us in his office.

This kind of amusement, displaying the foreigner, happened at the Nakamura's as well. I thought it was funny when ten-year-old Godzilla-chan brought several of his school friends at different times to stand in the garden outside the *tatami* room where Yuriko-san and I were sewing my summer kimono. One boy asked if I would give him one of my braids as a souvenir. Another said I looked like a strange kind of Heian princess. To spare my feelings, Yuriko-san would not translate all their comments telling me they were the remarks of children and too foolish to repeat.

My first day at the Nakamura's, I thought Godzilla-chan was a monster dressed in short pants and rubber shoes. He kicked up stones that shot like missiles out of the cloud of dust he created on the dirt road leading to the house with a telephone where I was being taken to call Aunt Elizabeth and report my safe arrival.

Godzilla-chan would address me as *ne-san* or "older sister" and impatiently but gently pound on my arm whenever I was too slow in turning my full attention to him. The first morning after my arrival, he wanted me to watch him crack a raw egg over his bowl of hot rice, add shoyu, stir it with *hashi*, and top it off with sprinkles of toasted seaweed. I copied every move he made and learned the Japanese word for delicious (*oiishi*) as part of that breakfast.

Throughout those ten days, he captured hard-shelled bugs, crickets, tree frogs, a bullfrog, and crayfish to show me. He, Yuriko-san, and I used hand motions for rock, scissors, paper, to decide who would be first in the game we wanted to play. They taught me nursery songs with hand motions, and if I did not get these motions right the first time, Godzilla-chan would grab my hands and move them along with his. We laughed a lot whenever he joined our games, and in spite of occasions when he reverted to a monster, I grew fond of "younger brother" and remember him with affection.

Watanabe-san, at thirty-three, can be as immature as Godzilla-chan, but he lacks the authentic charm of a ten-year-old who exaggerated the shape of his mouth to form Japanese words he wanted me to learn.

Sunday, September 27. I met Richard J. several days ago when we both returned home to the apartment building at the same time and entered the lobby together. He's taught Japanese history for the past twelve years at a Midwestern coed college and is spending the first six months of his sabbatical in Kyoto in order to read history with a professor at the university. In January, he and his family will move to Tokyo where he plans to finish the book he is writing.

I told him I was working on a translation and expected to be here until next June. He asked what I was translating. I told him.

"It won't be easy to find a publisher for that. Have you had other books published?"

"My thesis was published."

"What's the title?"

"Romances of an Old Order...."

He burst out laughing. "You lost academic credibility with that title. You probably had women reviewers."

"Actually, a male academic credentialed in Asian Studies gave it a favorable review."

He named local sights he, his wife, and daughter have seen or are planning to see before they leave. At the top of the second flight of stairs, he stated his question, "You're not married, are you?"

"No."

"I didn't think so. Nice meeting you."

"Thank you." Grandmother would have been proud of my forbearance.

Then late Friday night, a note was slipped under my door inviting me to an open house this evening in their apartment.

I was the first to arrive. (I admit I've been starved for company.)

Richard introduced me to Sarah, his wife, before telling me, "You mustn't let being a studious old maid prevent you from getting out of your apartment and enjoying your time here. Sarah knows all the museums and galleries, and she can help you find your way around."

He continued talking, either not noticing or ignoring the red flush on Sarah's face and how the two of us avoided looking directly at each other while he murmured on. How could a man who has taught twelve years at a coed college remain ignorant of capable women? I wonder if Sarah will call him on his arrogance when they are alone.

The doorbell rang, and he turned to answer it. Sarah took my arm and led me to a table beautifully laid out with appetizing food.

I started to say, "I really don't have time for...."

"Yes, I know, and I hope you won't think me rude and inhospitable..." She was hurrying to get it all out before we were interrupted. "...but I want to continue being selfish with the free time I have this year. When my children were little, I wanted to be home with them AND I have always wanted to study art. When my children started school, I took a part-time job for the extra money it would provide. I didn't take it for a challenge because there wasn't one, but working part-time got me thinking about ways to organize my time so I could go back to school and eventually work as a full-time, paid employee of our local museum.

"While Lisa is in school here, I spend mornings in museums or secret myself away in a coffee shop for several hours to read art history or take solitary trips to temples or explore parts of the city Richard has no interest in seeing. It's been wonderful to have so much uninterrupted time to pursue my interests—sort out what I really want. I plan to apply for a graduate program in art history.

"Richard didn't oppose my going back to work because the job wasn't a challenge to either of us, but when I get excited about being a student again and studying something I love, something that doesn't put him front and center, his insecurities bob to the surface. It's something we'll have to work out if I'm accepted in a master's program."

She told me their two teen-aged sons were enrolled in the American School in Tokyo, adding "...so far away" in a tone my mother uses when I tell her I'm going to Japan. Lisa, their youngest child, is well mannered, bright, and in the fourth grade at Kyoto International School. She adores her father who reciprocates with a story he has probably repeated on similar occasions for her benefit in which he tells how he and Sarah hoped their last child would be a girl and how she's turned out to be the icing on the cake.

Two elderly gentlemen who tip their hats whenever we meet in the lobby are German, teach architecture, and will leave Japan before Christmas. Their English is very good. One has a quirky sense of humor that kept all of us laughing.

A couple from France, who married just before coming to Japan, came to the party. They are here for only three months. She was hesitant to use English although I could tell she knows it quite well because her response to introductions and the German professor's humor, which he expressed in English, were quick and on the money.

I came back to my apartment rejuvenated by the evening's lighthearted conversation. An informal and convivial party like this leaves a pleasant aftermath.

Thursday, October 15. Sensei invited me to a moon-viewing party at a temple, and what a night it has turned out to be!

When he came to my office to invite me, I asked him to suggest an appropriate gift for our hosts. When he said "something American," I groaned inside. Where in Kyoto would I find something American that would blend in with those neatly wrapped boxes of tea, sake, or a good assortment of Japanese cakes that simplify the choice for Japanese gift-givers? And why did I ask him in the first place? I'm capable of making decisions on my own.

I spent the morning going from shop to shop within walking distance of my apartment without seeing anything indigenously American until I thought of combining a tin of Hawaiian pineapple with a fresh pineapple and a bunch of bananas—bananas because I eat them at home on American-made cornflakes—and three very large and expensive oranges probably imported from California. Sensei said to avoid extravagance, and in California, fruit is a modest and welcomed gift.

It took the greengrocer's wife twenty or thirty minutes to find a basket too large for my modest selection so we had to add another tin of pineapple and more bananas before she could wrap the whole arrangement in yellow cellophane. She wanted a large sale and her slow manner in negotiating the sale wore on my impatience until I would have bought the store just to get out of there. The basket was huge, weighing a little less than a ton. I shifted it up into both arms and found my way home through a screen of yellow cellophane.

Sensei asked me to meet another one of the invited guests at her hotel and to bring her with me to Kyoto station where the three of us would take a train to the temple. He told me she was an American manager of an art gallery in Tokyo and had come to Kyoto especially for this party.

On my way to the hotel, I mailed letters of application to coed colleges in California and the Midwest. I want a job in California, but I will consider the Midwest if it's offered. I want to secure a job by

April, although it may be too much to hope for. Mother urges patience when telling me to wait and see. I didn't want to wait and see when I was seven, and I don't now when I need a job to support myself.

Trina Sheffield was not difficult to recognize among other foreigners sitting around small tables in the hotel coffee shop where we agreed to meet. Others were sharing stories of their recent arrivals while waiting for the guide who was taking the group to a theater performance. Trina was sitting alone, oblivious to the others around her, staring into a cup of black tea. There was something about the way she was staring into her cup that made me think she was in love and thinking about "him." He could have been staring back at her because she's beautiful and that undoubtedly adds to his pride in her. Her good taste was evident in the dark-green dress she wore. She'd obviously considered the possibility of sitting on floor cushions at the party because her skirt was wide enough to cover her legs. I wore a russet-colored dress with a tulip-like skirt that adequately covers my legs when I sit sideways, and I'd braided russet and gold ribbons into a single braid.

Trina did not look up as I approached. I rustled the cellophane wrapping before I reached her table and introduced myself. I ordered a cup of black tea, and we talked about the uncertainties involved in gift giving.

"I have a friend,'" she said, "who rewraps flower vases, pottery, dolls, or whatever else she receives as gifts and cannot use and passes them along to someone else when it is her turn to give a gift."

"She must keep a record of who gave her what and when."

"She's clever; she would think to do that. You'll meet her tonight when she stops by the party. We were college roommates when she came to Boston to study architecture. She wanted to stay on in Boston after she graduated, but her parents persuaded her to return to Japan to consider a marriage proposal.

"The family who wanted her for their son and only heir owns a great deal of real estate in Tokyo. They wanted a daughter-in-law they could groom to eventually oversee the family's holdings and be clever enough to acquire more. Haruko thought additional classes in economics would be good preparation for such a large responsibility, and she persuaded her mother-in-law and the family to delay the marriage until she could complete a business degree at Stanford."

"Is the son mentally slow?"

"No, not at all, but being the treasured son and heir he was used to getting what he wanted when he wanted it. He had a big row with his parents when they refused to let him drive race cars. Apparently, his father's patience in persuading his son to the family's point of view won him over, and they've built their business on that rapport.

"Haruko understands the family business she married into; she works behind the scenes reviewing contracts, business plans, and whatever reconstruction needs to be done. She manages their busy social schedule, and they're considered a modern couple because they frequently entertain in their home."

"Do they have children?"

"A daughter. Haruko wants a son, of course. They both do. The pressure is on to produce a male heir, but even if they don't have a son, their four-year-old daughter already shows signs of being a capable manager."

"Professor Hiraizumi told me you were acquainted with the priest at the temple."

"No, I haven't met the priest. I know his younger brother, Shuji, an investment banker in Tokyo. Haruko introduced us when I came to Tokyo to open the gallery. He reviews the gallery's finances...banking and investments."

That almost imperceptible rush to say exactly how he was helping her made me think he was the man in her teacup.

I told her I'd visited temples as a tourist but not as a guest.

"The temple family we'll meet tonight has an interesting yet somewhat unfortunate story. Tadanobu, the priest and elder son, was thirty-nine when he took over as head priest after their father died unexpectedly. Two years later, Tadanobu's wife died while giving birth to their son.

"Shuji is Tadanobu's younger brother. Shuji married a woman from Kyoto who had left Kyoto only once before when her high school class took a trip to Ise Shrine. After she and Shuji moved to Tokyo, she developed a series of ailments that were difficult to diagnose and cure. One doctor they consulted said her illnesses were brought on by homesickness and might possibly be cured if she returned to Kyoto for an extended visit.

"Tadanobu's wife had died in childbirth, and the family decided Shuji's wife should come back to Kyoto to care for the infant and also help her mother-in-law with domestic responsibilities involved in running the temple. That happened three years ago, and she doesn't seem to want to return to Tokyo. Shuji comes to Kyoto occasionally to visit her and the rest of the family."

"Interesting," was all I could think to say.

We left the hotel to take a trolley to the train station. Trina told me she'd heard the Kyoto city fathers were planning to phase out many of these trolleys. A loss, I feel, since trolleys are a unique and enjoyable way of getting around town.

After we were seated, she asked what Professor Hiraizumi had told me about Kenichi Fujiwara. "Not much," I answered. "He did say Fujiwara-san is skilled in English, that he's an intelligent and sensitive interpreter of Japanese culture."

Trina and Kenichi Fujiwara became friends after Haruko introduced them at one of her parties. When he's in Tokyo, he stops in at the gallery to have a cup of tea with her or, if there's time, she orders sandwiches in. She went on to say, "Underneath Kenichi's admirable qualities and remarkable ability to get along with just about everyone, he's a very private person, what we in the States call 'his own man.' I've never met his wife, but they seem to have built a stable marriage. He takes his greatest pride in his two sons and hasn't liked being an absent parent this year.

"Since his father's death last year, Kenichi's taken on more responsibilities as head of their extended family. He's been asked to find a job in Tokyo for the second son of his mother's brother and more recently was consulted on another young relative's choice of a marriage partner. When I asked Kenichi how he manages sensitive family matters, he told me working in Kyoto this year has been a godsend because it's given him time to think. Maybe all that traveling back and forth on the train gives him space as well as time to sort through things.

"Kenichi has the alchemy of a poet when it comes to removing everything except simplicity and focus, something to remember when you talk with him about the diary you are translating. He also has a knack for refreshing mundane conversation; this, in addition to his intelligence and sense of humor, makes him a welcome guest at parties. Haruko sometimes says the success of the party she's giving that night or week depends on whether or not Kenichi will be there to charm the ladies. You'll find his attentiveness flattering, most women do.

"From the gossip I've heard, I gather he's been tempted into taking what's been offered by women who want to continue playing after the party is over. From what I know about Kenichi, I'd say these casual affairs, if you could even call them that, offer little beyond the play of sex. He's too clear-eyed not to recognize party games for what they are—games, and he's too ambitious not to move on when the game is over. I wouldn't know if his wife has heard gossip about those party games. I haven't met her so I have no idea how she would react to rumors of his infidelity."

(An insider's knowledge does add another dimension to Sensei's claim that Kenichi is a *sensitive*—or was it *skilled?*—interpreter of Japanese culture.)

At the station where Sensei, Trina, and I left the train, we walked in a crowd of adults and children, many wearing kimono, down a sloping road toward a lake where, on the farther side, the roofs of several temples were silhouetted against the evening sky. Sensei told us many years ago all these temples were under one roof, so to speak, that is until the government took steps to limit their growing political power; then they became "daughter" temples to be managed by individual priests and their families.

Loudspeakers piped folk music, adding to the festive mood. Vendors' carts lined an approach to a lakeside pavilion strung with round red paper lanterns glowing like rubies.

A smiling, kimono-clad woman met us at the gate of the temple and directed us to the side wing from which the outer walls facing the courtyard and the inner sliding partitions of large rooms had been removed to make an open and spacious gallery or porch. A lively and friendly party was already in progress. Some people were seated on cushions at low tables while others were moving around the room greeting those who remained seated and the new arrivals crossing their path. Gifts for our hosts were being left at the edge of the porch where it was easy to see most of them were the square and rectangular wrapped boxes that are the standard for gift-giving occasions. I left my cellophane-wrapped offering near those boxes, glad to be rid of its weight.

Tadanobu, the temple's priest, welcomed us at the edge of the porch and escorted us to an empty table with cushions piled underneath out of the way of other guests. From our table, we could see the far end of the room near the lake where tall grasses and plants grew higher than the railing. A wide expanse of evening sky was framed between the walled side of the room and a building post on the opposite side. The moon could not be seen from the table where we were sitting.

Sensei was disappointed when Trina and I chose to begin with soft drinks. After he saw we were comfortable, he excused himself to join another table where sake was turning everyone there into red-faced extroverts.

Looking around the room, I asked Trina, "Is that Shuji in the dark blue kimono?"

She gave a low, affirmative response, as if a louder voice might call him to her side. We had walked between and around several tables before we reached ours, so he would not have missed her arrival. It would take a more disciplined heart than his to not connect immediately with the affection that binds the two of them together or to not be pleased with the elegance she brings to a room.

"Has he spent time in the States?"

"Two summers, at special business and language programs."

He has a ruggedly handsome face. The kimono he was wearing enhanced his slight build, dramatizing the man who wore it. In traditional dress, he looks more like the wise, all-knowing, all-powerful samurai who, in the movies, saves the villagers from bandits. As soon as he could excuse himself from other guests, he made his way to our table.

Something about the way he engages Trina with his whole being tells me he is in love with her. Because he is still legally married to wife number one, inviting Trina to this party may have been their agreed way of letting her see for herself how things really are before she commits herself to a long-term affair that has little chance of completing itself in marriage. She is moonstruck and will accept such an arrangement because her better judgment can be held in abeyance as long as she and wife number one live in different cities.

A faint blush rose on Trina's face when Shuji said, "I am happy both of you were able to come tonight. We've held moon-viewing parties every year for as long as I can remember. During the war, parties were quieter and included only a few guests, and my father enjoyed sharing sake, singing old songs, and reciting poetry with friends. It's a tradition we all enjoy."

A few minutes later, he left our table to greet guests just stepping up onto the porch. Other people came to our table, introduced themselves, and stayed a few minutes to talk. Whenever there was a lull, Trina's gaze settled on Shuji's back and he would turn to hold her gaze before he excused himself from other guests and found his way back to her.

Shuji and Tadanobu's mother, Mrs. Shirakawa, came to our table to add her welcome. She has a flawless complexion, a broad jaw, and a bow-shaped mouth, and she knows how to make the simplest story entertaining. After she moved on to another table with three lively men, her face brightened to reflect the playfulness of those guests. Each man in turn, on seeing his face so well displayed in such a flattering mirror, vied with the others to keep himself the center of her attention. Mrs. Shirakawa is too practiced in her art not to be pleased with the effect she had on these men.

I used to think the modern version of the kimono stiff and restrictive until I watched Mrs. Shirakawa gliding around the room with a low sense of direction somewhere around her knees. I saw, as I am sure those men did, how seductively her kimono emphasized the bend at the back of her knees and how it rounded out her buttocks when she lowered herself to the *tatami* to sit with guests.

Shuji's wife, Fujiko, has a classically beautiful face and the obsequious manners suited to an idealized portrait of Japanese women, one that is propagated in TV soap operas and movies. She bowed her head to the floor in welcome when she brought a plate of freshly cooked food to our table. Trina inhaled the woman without a blush as all her attention focused on the woman she intended to or already had displaced in Shuji's affection.

Tadanobu's son, Ji-chan, had been trailing after Fujiko as she moved around the room serving guests. He caught up with her while she was sitting beside our table and backed onto her lap to rest from the stress of having to share his aunt-mother with too many people at one time. She smoothed his hair back from his moist forehead while she talked with us and pressed her cheek to his head just before she put him aside to stand up and return to the kitchen to bring food to other guests. Ji-chan was not happy with this. He grasped what he could of her kimono in his small hand and held on as they walked together along the verandah leading to the kitchen.

There were several other small children at the party besides Ji-chan. One of them ambled to a vacated table and drank whatever was left in untended glasses and cups before winding his way back to his mother and falling asleep on the tatami beside her. Throughout the evening, Ji-chan followed Fujiko around the room unless someone distracted him with a small toy or an enticing bit of food. Every now and then, when Tadanobu could manage it, he would capture his son and encircle him with his arms and legs while he sat talking with guests. Ji-chan would lean contentedly against his father until he spotted Fujiko, then he would struggle to free himself and go to her.

The group of red-faced men Sensei had joined earlier had been taking turns standing up and reciting poetry until, many cups of sake later, they were giving their recitations from a seated position.

Before the moon reached its zenith, another group of guests arrived.

"It's Haruko," Trina said.

"And her husband?" I asked, marveling at the tall, well-born man standing beside her.

"No. It's Kenichi. You didn't know he was coming tonight?"

"Sensei forgot to mention it."

So this handsome, self-possessed man was Sensei's capable chief assistant and designated go-between, the one Watanabe-san has been earnestly trying to replace and cannot. Now I understand why he cannot.

As Kenichi and Haruko wound their way toward our table, stopping to shake hands or bow and exchange greetings with other guests, Trina said, "How fortunate you are to be working with someone as knowledgeable and as interesting as he is. I'm sure you'll like him."

I already did. The full moon had pulled the thought up from the deep and left it at the edge of my awareness. Introductions were made easier by Kenichi's naturalness and the fact that he, Haruko, and Trina were old friends and comfortable together. During the lighthearted banter following our introduction, I thought he was sizing me up, trying to figure out from first impressions if working together was going to be pleasant or problematic. He's careful and reveals nothing.

Not long after she joined our table, Haruko excused herself saying she was expected at another moon-viewing party. She greeted several people on her way back to the edge of the porch where she stepped down into her shoes before turning back to exchange bows and goodbyes with Tadanobu and his mother.

We had yet to see the moon, so Trina, Kenichi, and I moved closer to the porch railing near the lake to appreciate its fullness. We sat there holding our faces to the breeze rippling the grasses near the porch. With the hum of other guests behind us, we could hear individual voices of people in boats out on the lake calling to one another and laughing. Kenichi told us these people wanted to see the reflection of the moon on the water; he called it a double moon.

As the party came to a close, we drifted toward the gate repeating our thank-yous, goodnights, and goodbyes to our hosts and convivial guests making the most of these last few minutes. Droves of people were walking past the temple up the road to the train station. Easing through this throng of people was the taxi Tadanobu had ordered for Sensei and another man less drunk than Sensei. The other man soberly promised to make sure the professor got home. Kenichi said he would see Trina and me home, and the three of us joined the crowd of people walking up the hill to the train station.

We said goodnight to Trina in the lobby of her hotel.

We walked the rest of the way home since the apartment he shares with Watanabe-san is on the opposite side of the campus from mine. The air was pleasantly cool after the crowded train, and there were not many people on the street. Most moon-viewing parties had concluded or were trying to conclude. We stopped awhile on the bridge to watch a small group of men on the veranda of an inn overlooking the Kamo River who appeared to be doing everything and anything to delay the inevitable end of their party. I could understand their reluctance.

Kenichi reminisced about the three years he and his family spent in Boston while he was studying for an advanced degree. His sons attended elementary school, and he is proud of the way they learned English, made friends, and adapted to America. In retrospect, those years now seem to him more like an extended holiday than three years of graduate school. He and his wife talk about returning to New England sometime in the future, perhaps after their sons have finished college.

When his work requires him to live someplace other than Tokyo, his wife remains at home so their sons' schoolwork will not be interrupted. She and a few of her former college classmates have organized a group for the purpose of studying the history and culture of the British Isles. She and Kenichi are planning to take a trip to England after both boys are in college.

When I asked if he had pursued this assignment with Sensei, he told me he had pulled every string he could in order to return to Kyoto for several months. (He's worked with Sensei on other projects that required only weekends in Kyoto.) Sensei's stomach cancer was diagnosed not long after they started work on their current project, and Sensei talked about immediate retirement. Kenichi persuaded him to stay on as he thinks purposeful work may extend Sensei's life, if only by a year.

Kenichi said, "My reasons for wanting to be here this year are far from altruistic. I don't like being away from my family for long periods of time, but I've wanted time for myself. It may be my last opportunity to work on or through personal questions until I become an old man with nothing to think about except the past and the hereafter. Working here with Sensei is giving me time and space to reevaluate the kind of personal freedom I found so liberating in Boston."

Before we said goodnight, we made plans to have lunch together on Monday to talk about how to proceed with the outings Sensei thinks will support my work on the translation.

I walked up the steps to my apartment thankful Sensei had not chosen Watanabe-san as the number one go-between. He could have. He might have thought it would be what Watanabe-san needed to develop greater confidence with English as well as practice the better part of working with a female colleague. Sensei may have reasoned that if Watanabe-san and I worked together it would help us both work through our initial negative response to each other.

Sensei picked up on my lack of enthusiasm when he called meetings with Watanabe and me in his office. The first time the three of us met together, I thought I'd been assigned the part of a voiceless body because Sensei directed all but one of his comments and questions to Watanabe, and the boy amazed me when he came up with a mature grasp of a situation or an insight that sprang free of effort. I had to change my attitude after that meeting because Sensei obviously knows Watanabe-san well enough to have scoped out the boy's potential and wants to groom him for a university position with greater responsibility.

The conversations Sensei and I have in the tearoom while reviewing a page or two of my translation are freer and have my full attention because he directs what he is saying to my work and life. The wealth of information and insight he offers can be quite playful, and time passes all too quickly. I leave the tearoom hoping I'll be able to plunder these conversations again when I'm back in the States and needing to recall focused instruction.

It's almost 3:00 a.m. I will stay up to see the sunrise. I need the sun to erase a night with such a full moon; my knees buckled, although I was sitting down at the time, at my first sight of Kenichi. I need sunlight to clearly see the landscape surrounding his home in Tokyo and mine in northern California.

Tonight, I was ambushed by love for a man I have known since time began and just met this evening at an unforgettable moon-viewing party.

Monday, October 19. When we are alone, we are Kenichi and Marina, not Fujiwara-san and O'Brien-san. During our walk home after the party, he asked if we could be informal when we are together and use first names. There is an ease between us, and not just because we prefer it so. It's as though we have always known each other, and he seems as eager as I am to know what the other was doing while we were living in different parts of the world.

At lunch, he told me he'd read *Romances of an Old Order.* He said he thought my imaginative faculty (his words) is capable of envisioning those areas of Kyoto we might not have time to explore together.

"Did Sensei assign my book as preparation for your assignment as go-between or did you read it because you were curious?"

"Both."

He told me they discussed my book, but he didn't say what Sensei thought about how I had developed my thesis or anything about the conclusions I had drawn from my study. I didn't ask, preferring to hear it from Sensei.

(Now I know eight people have read my book: my mother and father, my two friends and fellow teachers at Southern Women's, Aunt E., Kenichi, and possibly Sensei, although he may have gleaned necessary points from discussion with Kenichi and left it at that. Uncle Arthur reads history almost exclusively and because he was disappointed, and said so, when I changed my major area of study to literature, a strong sense of family loyalty prompted him to read my book.)

Kenichi told me he wanted to meet me after reading my book.

"Why? What did you find in it?"

"An appreciation of Japanese literature."

"That would be a given in my case. When a man as knowledgeable as you are reads my book, I want him to understand something he may not have realized or understood before, something that does not diminish his view of the world but enlarges and regenerates his hope for it."

"You aren't going to let me coast are you?"

"Do you really want to during the time you've set aside to explore life's more persistent questions? Besides, I have less than a year to work with Sensei and to learn what he can teach me about *Mountain Temple Woman.* If you and I are to work together, I would like you to be as honest and forthcoming as he is."

We talked about places in the city I had seen earlier in August. We discussed a number of places that might help me gain a better understanding of the woman's cultural, geographical, and spiritual supports. He wants us to take day trips to nearby mountain temples and to Nara. He wants me to try various foods as they come into season, and he knows restaurants that use traditional Kansai recipes.

His readiness to help makes me wonder how he imagined me before we met at the moon-viewing party. Aside from my appreciation of Japanese literature, he could have thought the occasional hour he'd been asked to spend with me would take too much time away from his real purpose in being here. I assumed we'd meet once or twice a month. He suggested we meet again Wednesday.

Living and studying in Boston must have helped him work through common Japanese assumptions that all Americans are crass, brash, incapable of understanding subtlety, and behave as though they owned the place, wherever that place might be. He most likely compared women graduate students he met in class with what he knew and expected from his wife and other Japanese women. I hope he was surprised and pleased by intelligent, incisive contributions those grad students made during class.

He would have met and observed other women at his sons' school PTA meetings, in restaurants and supermarkets, as neighbors in the apartment building where his family lived, as well as proprietors and other guests at the inns and hotels where his family stayed during weekend trips out of town. He seems to be the kind of man who'd pay attention to his wife's opinion about people she meets on her own.

As for myself, I can't say I was enthusiastic when Sensei said he wanted me to work with a go-between, someone I pictured at the time as an unhealthy combination of adolescent Watanabe-san and lecherous Akuma, but after today's lunch with Kenichi, I can say he is generous, thoughtful, intelligent, and very attractive.

Wednesday, October 21. As we were leaving for lunch today, Kenichi asked if I wanted to sample *dango*, a kind of rice dumpling that's often sold from vendor's carts and at festivals. I told him I did not always find the sauce to my taste. I said I preferred *ohagi* and the fresher the better. He said he knew where we could find delicious *ohagi*, and off we went into town and through a maze of back streets to a small, modest restaurant. While we were waiting for our order, I told him about my stay with the Nakamura's and that Yuriko-san had taken me to their village restaurant for my first taste of *ohagi*.

At this Kyoto restaurant, we were given a plate of three *ohagi*, one plain, one covered with soybean powder, and one covered with seaweed called *aonori*. The outer covering of the smoothly pounded rice was almost as soft as marshmallows. The bean filling was not overly sweetened or overcooked as there were soft chunks of dark brown beans to contrast with the smoothly pounded case of white rice covering them. *Ohagi* are delicious with tea and conversation with someone as interesting as Kenichi.

While we were talking about this and that, I got the feeling he had stepped back into himself to examine the moment. There's no need for either of us to try to impress the other, no need to pretend we are other than who we are, no need for credentials to establish position or ranking, no need to beguile or entice the other's interest. Our ease with each other was established the night we walked home from the moon-viewing party, or centuries before we met.

We could not find the right moment after lunch to end the pleasure we found in being together, and we left the restaurant to stroll through picturesque side streets. Near a canal, we walked into a shop where we were left alone to examine textiles and talk about traditional patterns woven into the cloth and the *e-kasuri*, the picture textiles the attentive proprietor brought out to show us as something a collector might be interested in buying.

We did not return to campus until late in the afternoon.

Evening. I've been looking through ads in the professional journals Mother forwards to me, and I'm getting more and more anxious about finding a job next year. I typed another formulaic letter in response to a newspaper ad Aunt Elizabeth had clipped.

I daydream about walking into a classroom to meet with students, some of whom will actually be interested in literature, and I get carried away with ideas for lectures and articles I'll write. In my daydreams, my articles are always published and result in invitations to lecture at professional meetings. Daydreams provide temporary escape from the fact I am not in as good a position as applicants living in the US who can be ready at a moment's notice to travel to interviews. The reality of my situation is not one of the two colleges that acknowledged my letters of application have given me the slightest reason to hope I will have a job next fall. So far it hasn't stopped me from trying; today, I mailed a response to the ad Aunt Elizabeth sent.

Saturday, October 24. We met this morning at Denachi-Yanagi station to take the train to Kurama. We planned nothing beyond a long walk to see and experience the hills.

As I approached the entrance to the train station where we agreed to meet, I saw Kenichi pushing pebbles around with the toe of his shoe as if he were trying to arrange them in some sort of order, and apparently, the stones weren't moving in the direction he had in mind. Arranging pebbles in some kind of order, like so many other things in his life this year, was giving him trouble. Did it have anything to do with spending the day with me? Our extended lunch hours in town established our ability to work together and how much we were alike in the pursuit of individual goals. What more could we discover in the hills?

When he looked up and saw me walking toward him, his shoulders relaxed and he warmed me with his smile. Trina was right about the way he focuses on the person he's with; it's immensely flattering to someone with my limited social life. His intelligence and good breeding, his sense of humor, fluency with language, and his appreciation and knowledge of the best in his country's art and literature do make him a perfect companion for a day in the hills...or lunch on a workday.

We left the train to walk along the road to a temple and farther on to a path that brought us to a thatched roof luncheonette where we stopped to eat. Nearby, ginkgo trees with yellow leaves were made more spectacular by the sun. While we waited for our order, we watched breezes move through a grove of young bamboo until that swaying band of green appeared to be playing at running up and down the hill.

We took our bowls of hot noodles to a table where we talked and laughed and out-waited the elderly couple at the table next to ours who were frankly curious about us.

"Is the foreign girl from Holland or Switzerland?" the man asked Kenichi in Japanese, assuming I wouldn't understand.

"She's from America," Kenichi told him.

"Really?" The woman was surprised. "American schoolgirls wear their hair in long braids like Japanese schoolgirls! I didn't know."

Kenichi turned his back to them, saying to me, "Let's not be distracted."

When the couple got up to leave, they bowed and wished us a pleasant day.

Kenichi pushed his empty bowl aside. "When you studied history, you read a great deal about my ancestors, now tell me something about yours."

"I haven't searched far beyond the short version we have at home and what I've found in history books. The ancestor who came to America in 1670 worked in some capacity for the king. Around or during my ancestor's lifetime, England had or was having major crises: There'd been a civil war and a period afterward when Cromwell ruled and the king was exiled. In 1665, there was another devastating outbreak of the plague in London, and the Great Fire of London destroyed a large part of the city. There were wars and rumors of war with the French and Dutch that unsettled everyone and extracted high taxes that left more and more people in poverty. Still, this particular ancestor of mine was not in such bad straits because he had a job and food to eat. He most likely wanted a challenge and the excitement and adventure and monetary reward such a trip offered.

"He took passage on a small ship housing probably as many as a hundred passengers. It took four to six weeks, depending on storms at sea, to cross the Atlantic. There'd be no fresh food except possibly milk from cows on board, and that was rationed or given to children and women who might be pregnant. The rest had to depend on beer or ale to ease their thirst. Maybe they collected rainwater to make tea.

"The worst part of life on board, at least in how I imagine it, is knowing there was no plumbing on board. The ship was crowded, with little or no privacy, so probably no one washed more than his or her hands and face, if that, and who but the most fastidious brushed their teeth? At night, the smell of unwashed bodies in cramped cabins would be nauseating. Body lice would have a free-for-all crawling from the seams of one person's clothing and matted hair to the other person sharing the bunk."

I shuddered at the thought. Kenichi couldn't hide a laugh.

"Another interesting thing about my ancestors for me personally is how much they resemble trees, especially oaks, in the way they moved across America to reach Red Oak, California. Oaks are the largest group in the family of beeches—which includes beeches, chestnuts, and oaks—They're all native to North America. When I was a child, I couldn't understand how my relatives could have different last names until I learned oak trees also have different names: northern red oak, white oak, scarlet oak, black oak, live oak, chestnut oak, and so on.

"Do you know oak trees are a symbol of strength and durability as well as beauty? The Druids and other ancient peoples considered some oak trees to be sacred. Oak lumber is used to build wine barrels, furniture, fence posts, and who doesn't admire doors and furniture made from oak. My grandfather thought northern red oak produced the most beautiful lumber. The town where I was born and raised was named for a northern red oak. How could I not feel related to trees?

"So, Kenichi," I concluded, "are you ready to take a test on O'Brien's unpublished study of her English-American ancestral history? You won't find what I've told you in a book."

He laughed, and I laughed, too. Laughing together made the afternoon golden.

We stood up to leave. He picked up a ginkgo leaf and gave it to me telling me in a mock professorial tone, "We also have oaks and a variety of other trees in Japan. During the Heian Period, white oak was used to dye the robes of noblemen in the third and fourth ranks. It was said the God of Leaves lives in the common oak.

"Do you know ginkgo trees, also called maidenhair, are native to China and Japan? They were exported to England thirty years before the United States began importing them around 1785. Once upon a time, ginkgo trees growing in courtyards of Chinese temples were considered sacred; however, this might have had something to do with the fact these trees grew near water and water was necessary when wooden temples caught fire.

"Ginkgo is the only surviving species of an order of plants thought to be over 250,000,000 years old. Nuts produced by female trees are cooked in tempura and puddings, and they can be roasted and eaten as you would peanuts."

I looked at the stem of the golden leaf I'd been twisting between my thumb and forefinger and burst out laughing. It would be hard to say exactly why we laughed or why we were overtaken by outbursts of laughter throughout the rest of this glorious afternoon.

Sunday, October 26. Talking about my ancestors yesterday is probably what triggered my dreams about Red Oak last night. I was a child again in both.

In the first dream, Mother and I were climbing the stairs to the attic. She held my hand while I lifted my short legs up to the next step. Then, while she was looking through the large trunk my grandmother used to store linens, I waited near the center of the attic to look at the tiered bamboo birdcage standing on a table. In my dream, this cage is the center display in an exhibition of treasures. Inside the cage, an energetic blue and white light I knew to be my grandmother darted back and forth. I've had dreams about the birdcage before. What made this dream different from earlier ones is my grandmother did not venture outside the cage to explore and rearrange the boxes and trunks as she had while she was alive.

A true fact about the birdcage is that one of my grandmother's friends, a widow, kept a menagerie of birds in her living room and sold them through advertisements in the local newspaper. My grandmother did not like keeping birds in cages; nevertheless, she was persuaded by affection and sympathy for her friend to buy both a cage and a bird. The canary did not live long after my grandmother brought it home. As soon as the bird had been buried at the far end of the garden, the cage was cleaned and taken up to the attic where it has remained unprotected by a dustsheet all these years.

My first dream started me thinking about how my mother and I both love our house in Red Oak in different ways. For her, it is the only home she has known, although she once thought she would move to another house after she married. For me, it was the best place to start my life with my parents and grandparents. Knowing my mother's love for the house and the work she puts into maintaining it, you might think she wants me to live there and continue preserving it. She doesn't, or at least she tells me she doesn't. She says what's important to her is that I finish traveling back and forth to Japan as soon as possible and settle down in the States, anywhere, as long as it's within the continental US. Fortunately for me, wherever I am, day or night, in memories or dreams, I can return to Red Oak.

In my second dream, my mother was preparing supper in the kitchen. I was in my highchair playing with wooden alphabet blocks my father was using to build towers and roofless houses I knocked down. The point of our game was apparently the laughter it provoked. In real life, my father probably built hundreds of these houses and towers for me before we outgrew that game and found others to play.

This dream reminded me of how easy it's been to leave rented rooms and apartments. I dismantle temporary living quarters almost as quickly as I knocked down towers my father built for me out of wooden blocks. I have had to move too often to want to hold on to more than a minimum of household possessions. Everything I own, or what is not stored in my bedroom or the attic in Red Oak, can be packed in boxes movers can carry out to a truck or I can mail from the post office.

My first week in Kyoto, I found little comfort in an unfamiliar apartment. The pillows I bought at the futon shop around the corner added no more than cushioning for the sofa's wooden arms. I put aside those feelings and looked elsewhere, eagerly finding my way around the city. One hot afternoon, I walked into the courtyard of a temple not far from Hyakumanben trolley stop in search of a shady place to recuperate from the heat. I stood near the gate in the glaring sun to watch a dark-robed monk whose feet were shod in white *tabi* cross a wooden porch and turn in at a doorway that led farther back into the temple. Young trees recently planted in the bare earth courtyard offered no shade. I decided to leave and spend some time, a lot of time, in an air-conditioned coffee shop.

On a stone bench, I saw what I thought was a pamphlet with information about the temple and walked over to pick it up and take it with me. It was, instead, an artful 1930s or 40s (I guessed) photograph of *Kannon*, the bodhisattva of mercy and compassion. If or when the person whose snapshot it was discovered it was lost, he or she would probably return to search for it. I was going to leave it on the bench until I turned it over and read the family name Nakamura on the back. It reminded me of the family who had given me a generous and kind introduction to Japan, and I claimed the photo as a good omen for the long, lonely year ahead. I brought it home where it now stands on the sideboard protected by the small frame I bought for it. Near the photograph, resting on a ceramic plate is the ginkgo leaf Kenichi gave me.

<u>Sunday, October 31</u>. Before I go to bed at night, I pull back the curtain that divides the bedroom from the living room so that when I wake in the morning I can look across the dining room and out the windows at the sky to check the weather. The days are getting shorter and cooler. If I wake before first light, there is time to prepare a Godzilla-chan-style breakfast of hot rice, raw egg, *shoyu*, and toasted seaweed. I eat at the table next to the window where I can observe how my neighbors across the street begin their morning.

Within minutes after the first wooden shutters are slid open, all the shutters on neighboring houses are opened. Bedding is flung over railings outside second-story windows, slapped a few times with a bamboo instrument similar to a carpet beater to release any reluctant human heat or dust and left to air. Not long after, umbrella-like frames holding small articles of freshly laundered clothing grow like mushrooms outside sliding doors. Morning is a productive time for these housewives. Their energetic example penetrates the concrete blocks of my building and makes me feel slothful if I dare stay in bed past 5:30 a.m.

I have come to appreciate and depend on the familiar view of tile roofs in the residential neighborhood stretching back beyond the individual houses closest to my apartment building. I find steadiness in this unchanging view whenever I get close to stumbling over an anxiety I don't want to explore at the time. I stare at the conformance in those tile roofs until I absorb the steadiness it offers.

I look back at my bed and the dark green nylon padded quilt I bought at the *futon* shop around the corner. The topside has a border of green surrounding a startling combination of large, nondescript purple, green, and blue flowers on a white background. I prefer the bottom side up as it adds an unbroken patch of green to that pale room. The quilt becomes a lily pad of exuberance whenever I throw myself back onto its silky material and roll around to stretch my arms and legs before drawing up into a lotus posture to consider my new position as frog princess in this developing tale of mutual love and longing.

Before my very human prince left on Friday to spend the weekend with his family, we walked to the Kamo River to have early morning coffee in a restaurant nearby. We stopped on the bridge to watch people walking beside the river. From our position in the middle of the bridge, we could see two other bridges spanning the river farther into town and beyond that, buildings partially obscured in what was left of morning haze.

How will I, I thought, be able to say goodbye in June when saying goodbye each time he leaves for Tokyo has me searching for words that might hold him here. We have become hesitant lovers. We do not speak of the love that is growing between us. We talk about architecture and art, our work and literature, and different areas of the city we are exploring together. We do not embrace; we sit together near a bower of golden leaves eating noodles, or we lunch in a small tea room on *ohagi* or go off to a restaurant far from campus to make two special hours of conversation. We do not kiss, we laugh. How frequently we laugh. There is such good humor in our affection.

He asked, "What are you thinking?"

"I was thinking about how my mother uses the expression, 'We will cross that bridge when we come to it' when we talk about a particular event looming on our horizon."

He did not respond.

"Do you want me to explain in more detail?" I asked.

"No, I understand."

"You and I do not speak about the bridge of words the two of us are unable to cross."

"We will not speak about it today."

"Why not?"

"Marina, when I go to Tokyo for the weekend, we both are confident I will return on Monday. When you leave Kyoto next June, we both know you will not return."

So he does think about our inevitable separation. Just a few days before while we were having lunch, I mentioned wanting to see the Heian Garden iris pond in bloom before I left.

He had said, "...The light will go with you."

"How you exaggerate."

He moved his head back and forth ever so slightly, and I knew he meant it as more than a compliment.

Kenichi only alludes to his feelings for me. Does he think if he doesn't express those feelings openly, he'll manage them better? I can't fault him about not opening his heart to vulnerability and uncertainty since I can't stay here when my grant year ends. What I want to talk about is how to manage the feelings we are now trying to ignore.

We said goodbye on the street outside the coffee shop, and I returned to my apartment thinking about our eager hellos and reluctant goodbyes, our hesitancy to touch and our inability to pull apart. I thought about the polygamous affairs, if they could be called that in the early century when *The Tale of Genji* was written, when a married man with a principal or official wife decided to take a secondary wife.

All principal wives were chosen from the courier class, and the greatest coup of all was to marry an emperor's daughter, which Genji did. Whether the chosen woman remained with her parents or was housed in a more secluded spot or in a separate wing her lover added to his house specifically for her, women who loved Genji were sure to hear about the woman who had so recently captured his heart.

In the novel, Genji is described as an ideal lover because he treated his lovers kindly and continued to show interest in a woman after his passion for her faded. To lose the interest of a sympathetic, persistent lover does bring a woman to a period of reckoning with her dashed hopes for sustaining the affair; it motivates her to examine her illusions about love and the ideal she's attached to her lover.

When a woman recognizes her lover's indifference or hears about his involvement with another woman, this all-too-human woman is brought face-to-face with anger, resentment, jealously, or grief—whatever range and degree of emotional expression her nature generates. She may consider revengeful thoughts, if only to relieve her distress. She may make a purgatorial attempt to pass through a labored stretch toward clarity to reach a kind of quiet resolution. If the woman's family responsibilities are minimal and if she is allowed to do so by the male members governing her family, she will renounce her interest in worldly affairs and take religious vows. During this initiation ritual her long, floor-sweeping hair will be cut short, at least to her shoulders. Then she and a few select ladies-in-waiting will retire to a nunnery or some other such removed and protected place.

Lady Murasaki is a poetic realist. She does not let us forget that every manifested form of creation is subject to change, the freshness of the morning glory, the plum blossoms that herald the spring, the cold moon that passes in the night; autumn grasses that die are blown over in the wind to disappear again into the earth. People grow old. Passions fade. Genji dies. The world is not the same without him, but life goes on. The people who knew Genji look back at the time when their ideal was embodied in his many noble traits. And later, when they think about the past and the many changes that have taken place since Genji's death, they discover that they, too, have changed…are changing.

Our love for each other has changed…is changing us.

Tuesday, November 3. There are many things I like about going to bed the night I wash my hair. After drying my hair with a towel, I comb it back and tie it at intervals with ribbons to enjoy its looseness whenever my movements cause it to swing across my back. I make the bed with the sheets and pillowcases my grandmother used to teach me embroidery. It's easy to spot my nine-year-old stitches in the yellow pansies alongside my grandmother's beautifully worked row of purple, wine-red, and blue pansies with green leaves. After we'd finished embroidering these bed linens, they were washed and ironed, wrapped in tissue paper, and placed in the attic in my grandmother's trunk of linens to be reclaimed by me when I married.

I open the living and dining room windows to let in the cool, damp night air and the sounds I try to identify as I'm falling asleep, and I push back the curtain between the bedroom and living room as far as it will go to give these sounds a clear path of air to my bed.

It is lovely to stretch out in the middle of my clean bed and place my cascade of partially damp hair over one pillow before I touch the embroidery on the top sheet to see if I can distinguish my grandmother's stitches from my own with just the tips of my fingers. The back of my head rests between two pillows while I wait for traffic lights on Higashiogi Street to jump over the houses on the street below and rapidly skate across the top of my bedroom wall in long rectangular strides before drawing up into a square and then disappearing altogether in the darkest corner of the far wall.

I wait for the sound of the trolley as it rolls up the street. I imagine the few weary passengers riding this late trolley, people now eager to be home and as comfortable in their beds as I am in mine. My eyes close to listen to the sound of sandals slapping the street as someone moves past our building on his way home. Later, what I guess to be a hard-shelled or large insect hits the screen covering the living room window. In the quiet that has settled over our neighborhood, I hear the whirring of its wings. On summer nights, I listened to cicadas, but now it's the chirruping of a hardy cricket that accompanies my descent into the silence of a dreamless night.

Saturday, November 21. I don't always eat breakfast at home. After working late several nights in a row, I walk to my favorite coffee shop near the Kamo River for a leisurely breakfast. The movement of people in and out of the coffee shop inspires me to write more descriptive letters home, and I usually take one or two letters to answer. Today, I brought the brocade book and have taken the booth farthest from the door to continue writing the unresolved story of Kenichi and Marina. If my narrative concludes before the holidays, so will this diary. By then, I'll have only a few empty pages left to fill. If we begin to talk openly about our love for each other, I may buy another diary in which to continue.

The Dutch Blue Coffee Shop has a clean, well-spaced interior with additional tables in a small room beyond the booths. The young waiter who serves my booth knows when to conclude a welcoming conversation and leave a customer to her coffee and thoughts.

The coffee beans used in this shop are freshly ground and brewed to order. The delicious aroma of coffee drifting out into the street pulls in more customers than any written advertisement. American, Vienna with delicious whipped cream, and really strong espresso are just a few of the coffee specialties listed on the menu. A white mug is used to serve American-style coffee; tiny cups are used for espresso, a flowered cup and saucer of European design for Vienna, and so on down the list. The type of cup in front of a customer is the obvious clue as to which brew has been ordered.

The breakfast specialty here is scrambled eggs served in a bowl of bread made by hollowing out the soft center portion of a small round loaf. It's an unusual way to serve scrambled eggs and belongs in the same memorable category as the potato salad sandwiches I used to eat when I was a student in Tokyo. I ordered those sandwiches not just because I was hungry and they were inexpensive and delicious, but also because no matter how many times I ate them, which was quite often, I could never quite digest why someone would put potato salad between slices of bread.

Today, while hunched over a mug of freshly brewed American coffee and waiting for a crusty bowl of eggs, I thought about Kenichi in Tokyo this weekend with his family, and how, after he returns, he will avoid coming to my office until his need to see me brings him around to ask about lunching together. He tries to keep our reunion formal, distancing himself as though we had met only once before and just briefly in a reception line at the embassy. I want to extend my hand and say, "How pleasant it is to see you again, Mr. Ambassador." His formality disappears in an onrush of affection for me that softens the stance of his body and brightens his eyes while he's looking at me. Perhaps he uses his weekends in Tokyo to strengthen his resolve not to be swept away, but when he does return, his longing for me emerges in spite of his resolution not to be drawn in.

He is fond of his wife. No, fond is too limiting a word, as his feelings for her are much deeper than that. There is a bond of honor and trust as well as affection between them. His wife is his good friend who added a great deal to their memories of what now in retrospect, seems like idyllic and carefree years in Boston. She is a major, dependable part of his life, a part he cannot and will not put aside. She is the mainstay of the home they have built together for their children, and she keeps him and their sons happy and productive. He is not certain I understand this because he stops short of discussing it openly with me, preferring to allude to his duty and responsibility as the father of two sons and head of his extended family.

He struggles with his feelings for me, but they haven't gone away. Maybe struggling with them is not the way to deal with them. If he moved back to Tokyo permanently and never saw me again, his memory of me would fade. Or would it? Would he regret not exploring a love he cannot shake off or hide from himself? He doesn't say if his weekends in Tokyo are helping him find an answer. I review and record what I see happening between us.

We do talk about other interesting things. His ego is not so needy he has to push my contributions aside in order to have the final word. He listens to what I say and elaborates the point, expanding it further. I can almost bank on the things we talk about at lunch developing into or opening other ideas when I am back in my office or while I'm working at home in the evening.

We went to Nara last Sunday. Every temple we chose to visit was congested with sightseers, every path swollen with families making the most of a beautiful day. Even the bus we took back to the train station was packed. I was wedged into the middle of the aisle without a strap to hang onto and barely enough room for my feet. When the bus lurched and jerked those of us in the middle onto other people standing in the aisle, Kenichi put his arm around my waist to steady me. Just as quickly, he released me. An uncontrollable giggle rose in my throat. I turned around to ask if he had burned his arm, but when I saw he had withdrawn into himself, I knew not to joke.

He avoided me until Wednesday when he came to my office in the guise of the ambassador. I wish he would spare me demonstrations of how he is working on burnishing his armor and shield. I excused myself from lunch saying I had errands that couldn't wait. I decided to work at home until after he left for Tokyo.

He called Friday morning from the train station to ask if I were ill. I told him I could concentrate better at home. It wasn't true, I had been reading the same paragraph over and over trying to get those few lines to register on my conscious mind when the phone rang and made me jump. The silence that passed through the connection between us told me he knew I'd been avoiding him.

"Let's look for antique blue and white china when I return. It's something you've wanted to do."

"Yes, that would be lovely. I'll look forward to it and seeing you again."

His voice deepened to his usual degree of masculine confidence before we said goodbye.

It's time I talked turkey with Ambassador Fujiwara. Sitting in the Dutch Blue Coffee Shop and writing my view of things in the brocade book is not going to resolve our dilemma.

Wednesday, November 25. Early this morning on my way to the office, I happened to see Kenichi and Sensei standing in an open area of campus they were making their own with the intensity of their conversation. Kenichi's head was bowed toward Sensei so as not to miss a word his mentor was saying. Both were wholly absorbed, a trolley could have rolled across campus beside them and they wouldn't have noticed.

Seeing them together like that made me wonder what might have crossed Sensei's mind yesterday when he came down the hall and saw Kenichi and me just back from lunch and still caught up in what we had to say about *The Makioka Sisters*. We had not seen Sensei walking toward us until he appeared at the same moment Kenichi and I stopped in front of my office door. Sensei had been ready to leave for home and was looking for Kenichi, something about revising the project's timetable.

Sensei is too keen an observer not to have noticed Kenichi and I were oblivious to everyone and everything except each other. It must have been as apparent to Sensei as it is to me that Kenichi and I turn toward each other as if toward a light.

If Sensei noticed that halo of light, was he making himself available and open to whatever Kenichi might have to say about the time he and I are spending together? If not yesterday after lunch in Sensei's office, then this morning on that spot of campus yard? What better place than open air to unburden one's mind.

When Kenichi came to my office today for lunch, I suggested we walk to Tanazaki's gravesite before deciding where to eat. I wanted to talk openly, and the cemetery was a better option than a crowded restaurant. We could start by continuing yesterday's discussion about my favorite Tanazaki novel and the lengthy process of finding a suitable husband for the third Makioka sister. In a recent reread, I was again impressed with its familiar human qualities. There are four Makioka sisters: the oldest is more tradition bound and less flexible; the second generous-hearted sister takes on the responsibility of arranging the third sister's marriage; while the fourth and youngest sister defies family standards to have a series of love affairs that result in a child and eventually marries a man who doesn't measure up to family hopes and expectations.

Yesterday, Kenichi and I spent most of our lunch hour talking about the third sister's reluctance to marry and what we each thought about her marrying someone she barely knew, although each prospective husband would have been recommended by the marriage broker or go-between after investigating that man's family, financial, and health history. A similar history would have been presented to the prospective husband's family for their consideration before final decisions were made.

Today, while we were walking to the cemetery, Kenichi wanted to talk about *Some Prefer Nettles*, Tanazaki's novel about the dissolution of a marriage. Tanazaki writes about how the marriage in this story comes apart when the husband and wife are no longer physically attracted to each other and find little else in each other on which to build interest or reason to continue their marriage. Their inability to act on what they know about themselves and each other keeps them from pursuing a divorce, although the possibility is discussed. At the end of the novel, they are still married and indecisive.

It made me think about Shuji and Fujiko, his legal, official wife, and how they've managed to live apart for several years. Fujiko appears to have a rewarding and productive life in Kyoto with her nephew-son and helping with household chores. By now, wouldn't parishioners consider Fujiko to be Tadanobu's unofficial wife? Shuji and Trina now live together in Trina's apartment in Tokyo, and their arrangement is certainly not platonic; nevertheless, Shuji's official address is the house he bought when he married Fujiko. The family apparently finds these arrangements workable for the time being at least.

Kenichi aligned himself with Tanazaki's mindset in these novels when he said, "My generation of modern Japanese prefer to hint at their feelings rather than declare them openly."

"Are you saying you want to continue alluding to your feelings for me rather than acknowledge them openly? Are you telling me the words I want to hear you say are a barrier you cannot or will not cross?"

"What concerns me is the toll we'll have to pay if I cross that barrier."

We reached the gate of the cemetery and entered to find ourselves alone on the wide gravel path inside the entrance. There were no other visitors arranging flowers or lighting incense in front of stone memorials, which, in this area of the cemetery, are grouped together on raised ground surrounded by a low stonewall about three feet high. The sky had been overcast all morning with intermittent sprinkles of rain. Perhaps the weather and maybe the lunch hour kept people away. The wall in front of Tanazaki's memorial was dry enough to use as a bench.

I brushed aside some gravel. "Let's sit here."

We have never been this alone, except perhaps for the few minutes he might stand in the open doorway of my office.

Kenichi took a seat on the wall several feet away from me and looked around at the gate, the empty gatekeeper's box, the ground under his feet, and down the path away from me.

"We can leave," I told him.

"No, we'll stay. You have something you want to say."

"This is a good place to talk. If I overstep the boundaries you've set or say something that embarrasses either of us, only ghosts who linger in this place will overhear."

He leaned forward resting his arms on his knees waiting for me to continue.

"When you stepped up onto the porch of the temple the night of the moon-viewing party and walked toward our table, the door of my heart opened spontaneously at the sight of you. Do you remember while we were sitting together looking at that full, heavy moon, you turned to look directly into my eyes? Perhaps you were taking my measure, but for me, it was as if you lifted me up out of the carefully constructed plans I've used to build my life and took me into a receptive room in your heart.

"Falling in love with you is dangerous, but it happened. The time we've been spending together has been wonderful; the danger lies in my wanting you to promise more than you can deliver. Until I met you, I never thought I'd ever fall in love with a married man; I'd never even considered the possibility. Yet in spite of knowing it to be unwise and undisciplined to entertain such thoughts, I continue to think about what it is to love you."

"Marina." His voice softened as he moved closer to me. "You don't have to say anymore, I understand. I knew I loved you from the moment we stopped on the bridge to watch revelers at the inn trying to delay the end of their party. I'm not as emotionally courageous as you are when it comes to voicing my feelings for you. I hesitate saying I love you for reasons other than what you might think.

"Do you understand the way we love each other is not to be compared to the way I love my wife and children or the way you will love the man you will marry someday? Both of us cannot forget we have families we care about and responsibilities we can avoid or want to abandon. Both of us have ambitions we want to realize. Tell me how you want to manage these next months, and I will do as you say, but don't say we can't spend time together. I would miss you."

"And I would miss you. We could make an effort to be more disciplined by taking lunch closer to campus. We don't have to take Saturday or Sunday excursions unless it's something I shouldn't miss, and we could limit the number of walks we take together…and you don't have to stop alluding to how you feel about me since I can live with those allusions now."

We laughed and stood up to leave. We found an almost empty restaurant on our way back to campus and took the booth farthest from the door. My happiness was such that eating a dainty cucumber and tomato sandwich presented on a clear glass plate and paper doily became another way of making love.

<u>Friday, December 18</u>. He came to my office this morning and for the first time, closed the door behind him and kept his hand on the knob. He was obviously distressed, and I expected the worst.

"What's happened to Sensei? He's been taken to the hospital?"

"No, no, he's fine. Sorry. I didn't mean to startle you. He's released me for a month to work in Tokyo, in my home office. I'm leaving today."

"How long have you known this?"

"A week."

"He knows about us."

"Yes."

"And?"

"And he asked me not to write or call you while I'm away."

"It's not unreasonable if he thinks uninterrupted time with your family will change your mind about me."

"Marina...."

"It's okay. At the moment, I can't see how your absence will change my feelings for you, but I'll manage it…somehow."

"Have you decided to spend Christmas with your neighbors?"

"Yes."

"I hope you have a pleasant holiday and not miss your family in Red Oak too much."

"It's you I'll miss, Kenichi. Let's wait until after you return to wish each other a Happy New Year. If you decide not to return, there's no way 1971 could be happy."

"I love you, Marina. Distance won't change that."

"I love you, Kenichi."

I've been sitting by the window of my apartment savoring our conversation as I write it. I'll need every word he said to survive the next month without him.

The sun is setting, and I don't intend to move from this chair until the last trace of sunlight has disappeared. Birds are settling on the bare limbs of that tall tree. With their round bodies perched on thin branches and their tails visible below, they look like a row of unused commas. Kenichi, Kenichi, Kenichi is the name I read between those commas. I opened a book, but all I could see was his face.

I'm going to take a long, hot shower, wash my hair, and put on the white, silky soft cotton knit pajamas Aunt Elizabeth sent along with the sage-colored bathrobe Mom and Dad sent for Christmas. I couldn't wait until the twenty-fifth to open their packages, and I can't wait until Christmas night to wear them.

Saturday, December 19. He came to me last night. I had gone into the kitchen to put water on to make tea and forgot to turn on the burner. I stood by the stove rubbing my wet hair with a bath towel thinking about him, as I had been all afternoon, when I remembered the ribbons I needed to tie back my hair were in the bedroom. I was tying the last ribbon when the doorbell rang.

"I wanted to see you again before I left" was his explanation.

"Come in, I'll make tea," I said, opening the door wider and then abruptly turning away, leaving him to close the door. I had been imagining him on the train, and his arrival at his house where he would close the *genkan* door and thoughts about me behind him before stepping up into the excitement caused by his homecoming. Seeing him here in my apartment was a confusing mix of disbelief and joy. I stood in the kitchen doorway watching him take off his coat. When I didn't move to take it from him or suggest where he could put it, he laid it over the back of a dining room chair.

He stood beside the chair looking at me. "Marina?"

"You didn't expect to find me in pajamas without my hair in braids."

"It's more than I dared to hope." We laughed but we didn't move.

"Why did you miss your train?"

"I can't leave until I know if, in spite of what may happen next June, you'll take a chance and love me as I want to love you."

"I will."

Monday, December 21. Watanabe-san is go-between again while Kenichi is away. He came to my office early this morning to tell me Sensei wanted to meet with me in the tearoom.

Watanabe-san has developed an expansive, possibly caring, attitude toward me and it adds an attractive bloom to his character. It appears in his assumed role of protective older brother who hovers like one who knows far better than the woman colleague who loves his roommate the destined end of her love affair.

Sharing an apartment with Kenichi gives Watanabe-san opportunity to observe what cannot be hidden during Kenichi's unguarded moments at home. Does Watanabe-san discern by the look on Kenichi's face when he returns from using a pay phone whether he has called his wife or me? I don't think Kenichi would discuss his feelings openly with someone as removed as Watanabe-san is from the heart of the matter, but that's not to say Kenichi wouldn't allude to things he might want or expect Watanabe-san to understand. More importantly perhaps for Watanabe-san is that he will begin meeting with possible marriage partners after the New Year. That's reason enough to observe Kenichi, maybe learn more about how a confident, secure man successfully woos a woman.

In Japan, the value of accurate information runs a close second to gold. Watanabe-san is intent on finding the gold in Kenichi's and my affair by sifting through what he's been observing for evidence of just how far we are taking it or have taken it. Today, he lingered in my office long enough after telling me the time to meet Sensei to let me know with a knowing smile that he knows the glow on my face has to do with more than just soap and water. Before Kenichi left for Tokyo, he had to return to their apartment to pick up the satchel he'd left by the door when he said he was going out to make a phone call. When he did not return to their apartment until just before dawn, Watanabe-san could be sure no telephone call had taken that long.

Before Kenichi left my apartment Saturday morning, after he'd dressed and I had wrapped myself in my robe and retied my hair, he put his arm around my waist saying, "Let's dance," and sang softly and well, *"You're Lovely to Look At"* by Jerome Kern and Dorothy Fields.

"Did you learn that in Boston?"

"Japan. College friends and I learned the scores of American musicals and how to dance. We wanted to be modern; it was hip and America was 'it.'"

"And now?"

"Now I know modern life to be disenchanting as well as good, and I find myself longing for the sublime."

We danced our way in between the dining room table and the sideboard where he picked up the ginkgo leaf from the plate near the photograph of Kannon.

"Where did you get that picture?"

"I found it in a temple courtyard."

He turned the stem of the leaf between his fingers. "Why did you keep this?"

"It was a golden day."

"It was golden. Whenever you look at it, know I have loved you throughout the past 250,000,000 years and will continue to love you throughout the millions of years to come."

I said, "Know that I love you in the wine you drink, the furniture you use, the posts that support the fence surrounding your house. Know that when you see a white, red, or any other species of oak tree, I am with you, loving you wherever you are."

Lovers' vows the morning after.

Sensei nodded to an attentive young waitress the moment he saw me enter the teashop. She came to our table to place a woven, lacquered box containing an attractive assortment of *okashi* on the far side of Sensei and then laid out the pottery plates and small bamboo picks we use to eat these delicate and decorative small cakes before she brought our tea.

"Today," Sensei said, "we are drinking *sencha*, a very good grade of tea, even so, care must be taken in brewing; if the water is the right temperature, it will take only a minute or two to steep. We practice economy by using the same leaves to make a second cup. To do that, we'd just wash the leaves." He demonstrated with his hands how he would swirl a teapot around to release the saturated leaves into more hot water. "We do not expect the same full flavor in the second cup;

nevertheless, it serves to slacken our thirst and contribute to our sense of well-being."

He lifted a cake from the lacquered box with the *hashi* (chopsticks) that had been placed beside the open box and put it on my plate before serving himself. He did not reach for a bamboo pick to cut a manageable portion of cake. I waited.

Before Kenichi left, Sensei had asked him again to use his time at home to consider the consequences of pursuing his passion for another woman. Such actions, he said, change the order of things and cause suffering. Sensei feels responsible for bringing us together; even so, as clear-sighted as he is, how could he have foreseen the possibility that Kenichi and I would fall in love? How could he have avoided playing his part in bringing two unlikely lovers together?

Kenichi told me when Sensei was a young man beginning his career at Kyoto University, his parents arranged his marriage to a suitable young woman. Around the same time, he unexpectedly fell in love with the daughter of an older colleague. That young woman apparently felt the same way about Sensei, although they both knew they could do nothing about it. For almost a year, she refused to consider marriage proposals a go-between brought to her parents. Her parents grew impatient with her and told her it was her duty to marry and she should resign herself to it.

Her parents were not unkind and sent her off to France where she studied while living with an aunt who had emigrated there. In exchange for this year abroad, she agreed to marry the man her parents chose for her when she returned to Japan. While she was in France, Sensei's wife died during childbirth. To make a long story short, Sensei and his beloved married after she returned from France and after an acceptable period of mourning for his wife had passed.

Sensei was much younger then and perhaps more impetuous; his passions, too, were no doubt stronger and not as well sorted out as they are now. He obviously lacked teaching experience at the beginning of his career, but he had enough sense to know the scandal of divorce would affect the advancement of his career. He wanted to avoid embarrassing his wife, since she would be the one to bear the community's curiosity and gossip about how she'd failed to please her husband, as well as the pity and tsk tsking of relatives and neighbors.

In the tearoom, Sensei covered my love affair with Kenichi in a less personal and more comprehensive manner.

"In Japan," he said, "the family is the heart of our nation. The foreign press has criticized Japanese men for not taking their wives with them to public functions or to foreign countries where they are sent to study, and we've been disparaged for not openly demonstrating our affection for our wives.

"It is apparent these Western critics do not understand the significance of a Japanese home. It is a man's inward-turning place. For this reason, he does not expose it or the emotions that are played out at home to public view. He may talk about these things with a trusted friend or family member, but he does not expose his home or his emotions to public view.

"As husbands, we have much to learn. We depend on our wives to be patient and understanding when we expose our weakness through careless or thoughtless behavior. Both husband and wife have to learn patience and tolerance. Many years ago, our divine ancestors enacted the drama of interdependence for our example. It is through remembering our divine ancestors that a man learns more about the qualities that make him Japanese, the qualities that make him a man, but (and here he paused to sigh) being human, we are weak.

"If a married man decides to act on his attraction to another woman, it disrupts the harmony between himself and his wife, between the parents and children. If the husband impulsively satisfies himself in momentary passion with another woman, his wife must practice forbearance. The husband will be indebted to her if she demonstrates patience and gives him time to rehabilitate himself.

"If the attraction a man feels for another woman is more than casual entertainment, if she becomes more to him than temporary diversion or relief from stress, he assumes responsibility for her. The law allows only one legal wife at a time; however, if a man willingly assumes emotional and monetary responsibility for another woman, he has, in effect, taken a second wife, and he is obligated to deal honorably with her.

"We would try to dissuade a man from making any such arrangement or taking on this added responsibility. We would ask him to consider how he might feel about this second woman when she becomes as familiar to him as his present wife. We would give him time to consider the consequences of his actions and the disruption it would bring to his family, as well as the energy and thought it would drain from his work.

"If his mind is set and we cannot deter him and he goes ahead with these arrangements, everyone concerned would hope the second wife remains modest and unassuming. The acknowledgement of her new role should not make her bold, nor should she put herself forward in an untoward manner or become a cause for embarrassment. Everyone concerned appreciates circumspect behavior."

I wonder if Sensei could tell by my face and my bearing the moment I entered the tearoom that Kenichi had not left on the early train.

Sensei cut into his cake and smiled, not at me, but at being able to eat something as special as *okashi* again. At the end of tea, after we both enjoyed a second cake, he asked the waitress to wrap the lacquered box containing the remaining cakes and then presented the package to me as a Christmas present.

Wednesday, December 23. I should stay away from the window and stop looking down at the street and the silent Japanese houses sheltered behind forbidding walls, but I can't pull myself away from the view, at least not for long. I brew more tea when distracting thoughts interrupt my work, and bring a cup to the window where I watch and wait for signs of life on the empty street below.

There has been no letter from him. There won't be as he said he would abide by Sensei's request not to write or call me; still, I continue to hope for reassurance of some kind—a picture postcard of Tokyo Tower would do. It has been five days since he left, and I wish there were a way of knowing whether or not he's thinking of me. Even better would be to see him walking up the street and turning in at my gate. He will return here in forty days if nothing delays his return. That's a very long time to find satisfaction solely in my work.

Missing the man I love is something new for me, but feeling lonely in Japan isn't. I'm more susceptible to loneliness in large cosmopolitan cities like Tokyo. It wasn't until I met Aggie at ICU that my view of that very large, overcrowded, impersonal foreign city changed to an exciting and interesting place to live and study. Her sense of humor and enthusiasm for things Japanese added a greater degree of adventure than I had mustered on my own. I wouldn't understand how lonely and depressed I would be without Aggie until I came back to my room after seeing her off at the airport and discovered my zest for living in Tokyo had left with her. Without her, the rest of my year in Japan was going to be as dismal as the view from the window of my tatami room.

While I was standing at the window brooding over her departure, I thought the only way I could survive would be to move back into the dorm as soon as a room was available. My courageous self, the one that imagines overcoming obstacles, raised doubts about a hasty retreat from the rooming house. After all, living as we had in a neighborhood where we absorbed what we could from everyday contact with our Japanese neighbors made me think returning to the dorm would be running away from the challenge of managing on my own. It might take a day or two, maybe longer, to not feel so desolated by Aggie's departure, but after that, I was sure I could come up with another option besides the dorm.

Previously, when I had stayed home to study and needed a break, I stood at that window and looked across fences and backyards of other nondescript buildings. The obligatory pine tree and rock had been added to several spaces originally designated as "gardens," but with changing tenants and time, those gardens filled with an overflow of household clutter. I usually focused on a second-floor porch in the row of ramshackle buildings that made up the horizon I saw from my window. That porch with its seemingly insecure construction appeared to be a hasty afterthought to the builder's original plans.

The porch was used as the tenant's laundry room and wasn't required to bear more than the weight of the petite housewife who came out early every morning to hang the laundry she took from the small washing machine placed just outside the sliding glass doors of her kitchen. While I was getting ready for school, I watched her snap out pieces of wet, twisted clothing and string them out in full proportions to dry on bamboo poles suspended under the blue plastic roof. As soon as the sliding door into the kitchen had been curtained off with trousers, children's shirts, undergarments, and light cotton kimono, I knew it was time to leave for class.

When it rained heavily or all day, she washed small articles such as her children's white stockings, a child's underpants, or thin cotton towels advertising Meiji or Morinaga milk given as gifts to housewives by local shopkeepers who appreciate their business. She clipped those pieces of hand laundry to an umbrella-like frame she hung just outside the sliding glass door where it was protected from a downpour by the blue plastic roof while it danced about in the wind accompanying the rain.

When it was time to secure the balcony door for the night, the umbrella apparatus and still damp hand laundry was taken inside and hung in the kitchen, or so I supposed, to dry. If those stockings and underwear did not dry overnight, they were returned to the porch in the morning. During the rainy season, stockings were sent back and forth from porch to kitchen and kitchen to porch until they were dry, or the woman grew exasperated and ironed them dry, as she may have done with the sheets and sleeping kimono she let hang for a two-day stretch.

The woman never gave herself a full day of rest. Sunday mornings, more often than not, she had washed an article or two and hung them out to dry before I was up and about. Family laundry was that woman's testament of industry and household habit.

The other woman I couldn't help observing while living at the rooming house was the plain, middle-aged woman who was responsible for the domestic upkeep of our building. Aggie and I nicknamed her Mrs. Tabemono (Mrs. Food) because she carried a supply of snacks in the pocket of her smock and fed herself out of this store throughout the day.

She was at the *genkan* in her sleeping kimono to welcome us home no matter what time we returned in the evening or how quietly we slid open the door hoping the rattle would not disturb her. If it was very late, we repeatedly bowed and apologized for disturbing her sleep although she alleged it to be no trouble at all. By the time we had our shoes off and were in the hallway ready to climb the stairs to our rooms, she had pulled out a small cracker or a piece of candy from the sleeve of her sleeping kimono and had popped it into her mouth.

She rarely took Sunday off to entertain herself as other women did with a shopping excursion to one of the large department stores. She didn't go to movies because watching television was more convenient and economical, and she watched soap operas whenever she could. The days I stayed home to study, the dialogue from these shows reached my room through poorly insulated walls unless her TV was turned down to a whisper, which it rarely was. She didn't speak of family or friends to us when we did chat briefly on our way in or out, and TV seemed to be the only company she entertained in her room. More than once, I wakened in the middle of the night when I heard what I thought was someone talking in the hall outside my room. As soon as I realized the sound was coming from Mrs. Tabemono's television set, I had no trouble falling back to sleep.

She was frugal, as were all the women in that neighborhood. They saved items that could be recycled to sell to the scrap dealer who came by periodically in a small, three-wheeled truck to buy bundles of newspapers, empty bottles, rags, neatly tied bundles of cardboard, and whatever else those thrifty housewives collected to sell for extra money.

It was the custom of the women in our neighborhood to return empty sake bottles to the sake dealer whenever they bought a full one. Mrs. Tabemono told us she did not drink sake, but she collected three or four one-and-a-half-liter bottles every week or so from the male students in our building who couldn't be bothered or had forgotten to return their empties. When Aggie and I saw her arranging crates of empty bottles in the backyard, Aggie made up a believable story about how our landlord encouraged Mrs. Tabemono to sell empty bottles and other recyclables for money she could add to her own purse. He wanted her to think this extra money was a reward for her unfailing diligence and loyalty and for not leaving the building unattended except when she had to go out to shop for food and other necessary items at neighborhood stores. If Mrs. Tabemono made additional money throughout the year by selling bottles and old newspapers to the scrap dealer, the landlord's conscience would sting less when he gave her a minimal year-end bonus.

A few days after Aggie left, I was in the bath, which was located on the first floor down a hall facing the backyard of the rooming house. I felt faint while soaking in the boiling hot water and got out of the tub to stand by a tiny window to breathe cooler air. I saw Mrs. Tabemono sitting alone on the narrow verandah outside her room smiling and bowing to an invisible guest. She picked up a cup of tea and held it with her left hand under it like a saucer and the four fingers of her right hand circled around to the front and her thumb around the back. After taking a ladylike sip, she replaced the cup on its cheap lacquered saucer and laughed and talked to an imaginary friend without uttering a sound. It was poignant to see how this lonely woman found a sympathetic, convivial friend with whom she could share moments of her life.

Mrs. Tabemono may have been talking with her friend about fresh blossoms on a plum tree that grew in the garden outside her room. She may have been sharing her pleasure in an extensive and well-cared for garden leading down to a pond stocked with colorful and expensive carp, or the women may have been watching a full moon hanging over the pond, but in fact, it was mid-afternoon and the area at the back of our building originally intended as garden space when the house was built was quite small, cramped, and dismal. With the crates of empty sake bottles and a stack of lumber kept for repairs, there was barely enough room in the remaining space for an ancient tree now supported by bamboo poles and with enough whiskery needles to identify it as a once vigorous pine.

A gardener, or someone known to the landlord, kept a haphazard collection of gray, oddly-shaped rocks in whatever space he could find in the yard until he came to haul one away and replace it with another. In spite of the cramped arrangement, the rocks were beautiful when a steady rain turned them black and individual shapes were more distinct.

I went back to the tub mulling over Mrs. Tabemono's pantomime and sat down in the hot water and forgot where I was or how long I had been there until one of the impatient male students shouted at me through the thin wooden door of the bath saying I had overstayed my time and threatened to come in and pull me out if I didn't get out immediately. I didn't stop to question whether he would carry out his threat and grabbed a towel to cover myself while I scrambled my wet body into my clothes.

Back in my room, I lay down on the tatami and stared up at the water-stained ceiling. The wide stain on the left resembled a mapmaker's view of the Baja Peninsula and the long, narrow, snake-like stain on the right reminded me of the Mississippi River. I looked from the water-stained ceiling to the tiny portion of blue sky visible at the very top of my window. I wanted another place in the city with a broader horizon, a place where I could take in more than the monotonous round of daily chores and unexpected exposures of Mrs. Tabemono's lonely life.

The next day at school, I read the advertisements for rooms pinned to the bulletin board. My search led me to Mrs. Matsui's house, her well-tended garden, the Ladies of the Bath in a quiet neighborhood that was protected, or so it seemed at that time and now in present memory, from the intrusion of heavy traffic and Tokyo's bustling streets.

<u>Christmas Day, December 25</u>. I spent the afternoon with Sarah, Richard and their three children. They're planning to visit Inari Shrine and the Moss Garden before they leave next Tuesday.

When Lisa left the board game, which she, the boys, and I were playing to help her mother finish preparing dinner, Richard took her place. The younger boy pretended he didn't see an obvious move so Richard could take it and win. The older boy hit the younger on the arm to let him know he knew he had faked it. It didn't surprise me to see siblings communicating this way. What did surprise me was how Richard claimed his win without acknowledging his son's help or thanking him. I waited for him to make a joke about it or at least include his sons with a laugh and a wink of his eye, but he didn't, and the boys didn't tease their father about how he'd needed their help to win. Their silence was puzzling.

Richard is irritating and condescending when he presumes the role of experienced advisor, assuming, of course, I'd be foolish not to take advantage of his expertise. Today, his advice was to tell me to consider another title for my translation because *Mountain Temple Woman* would be uninteresting to women readers unless I use the love angle again. I didn't ask the title of the book he's writing.

Sarah hopes to hear she's been accepted for graduate school while they're in Tokyo. She's going to take one or two courses next summer to get back into a disciplined habit of study. I wish her well.

It's Mother and Dad's turn to spend Christmas in San Francisco with Aunt Elizabeth and Uncle Arthur. After dinner, Dad and Uncle A. will talk in the living room about the war in Vietnam and California politics. Mother and Aunt E. will talk as sisters do in the kitchen while they clean up and put food away. Aunt E. will reassure Mother again about my personal safety while I am "so far away."

My memories of Christmas include the pleasurable hum of conversation and outbursts of laughter that added extra richness to the gravy and made popping a whole jellied cranberry between my teeth a game I could play by myself at the table, and an extra helping of stuffing, however small, was as necessary at holiday dinners as a period was at the end of a sentence.

How easily I return to Red Oak when I'm this far from home.

The mailbox remains empty of postcards or letters from Kenichi. I am not a major character in the domestic scenes being played out in Tokyo. Maybe it is better he doesn't interrupt his participation in his family's life to write marginal notes to me. If push comes to shove while he's away, he will not return to Kyoto. My first thought this morning was just that, he will decide to stay in Tokyo, and I will never see him again.

Tuesday, December 29. There wasn't much to write about last August except tourist jaunts, memories of earlier trips, and home. Meeting Kenichi changed that. Whether or not I will ever want to reread what I have written about finding love with him, I am going to record the rest of the year as it happens...or doesn't happen.

Today, I went to Sanjo to look for another diary with a cover as beautiful as this brocade one. When I asked to see what was available, I was shown pink flowery covers, cutely feminine cartoons, and tiny, repetitive brocade patterns offering no suggestion of something beyond the obvious. I got annoyed with not finding what I hoped to find in a city that's been known, at least in the past, to nurture traditional arts and crafts. My empty stomach helped me decide to settle for a student's spiral notebook and to stop for lunch in the first cafe I saw.

Food revived my spirits, and to get a fuller dose of holiday bustle, I joined the crowd of people in a department store shopping for New Year's presents. Everyone looks for the right gift at the right price for family, friends, and those to whom they owe a special debt of gratitude. There are counters stocked with specially wrapped tinned and bottled goods, imported liquor and wine, coffee, baskets of fresh fruit, and fish, of course, anyway you like it: fresh, smoked, dried, whole, fillet, or roe. Department stores will deliver these packages, and the gift not the giver makes a timely appearance in the recipient's *genkan*.

The fever of New Year's preparations is high in our residential neighborhood as well. My neighbors across the street have been cleaning their houses from top to bottom to be ready for the first three quiet days in January. In the covered street of shops and the supermarket, women are wooed and won by shopkeepers offering prepared food for sale, food these women will transfer from store wrappings to tiered lacquered boxes that have been packed away or kept on a shelf until the New Year holiday, or some other special occasion brings it to the table to be quietly admired.

Tasty tidbits of food will be offered to friends who step into a *genkan* with New Year's greetings and are asked to step up into the house for tea or a cup of sake. Conversation around these low tables will be lighter and less invidious than the usual neighborhood gossip. The guest who has a way of dusting off the staleness that clings to formal calls brings fresh air to the visit. The hostess will notice and appreciate the largesse in that guest's contribution.

Kenichi's wife has three man-sized reasons for happiness when she shops for their family meals. When she gets to the market, perhaps she'll discover chicken breast fillets are a better bargain than fish, especially if she has a recipe the whole family enjoys. Experience helps her choose the right proportions of red and white *miso* to make a winter soup, and she knows which pickle adds flavor to the last few mouthfuls of rice.

She and Kenichi will discuss their list of friends and his colleagues and the appropriate gifts for each. They will decide which of their New Year's calls requires their combined appearance in someone's *genkan*. They will be admired as a handsome, intelligent, compatible couple who have made a success of their marriage, a good home for their children, and who are proving themselves capable of addressing and managing their extended family's concerns, interests, and resources.

Heart of my heart, I stand outside your charmed circle and wait.

Monday, January 11, 1971. Sensei, Watanabe-san, and Akuma were away from campus during the holidays, and it's just beginning to pick up speed after a quiet and slow beginning to the New Year. Even today, people passing in the hallway can be heard offering the traditional congratulatory New Year's greeting.

This morning, Watanabe-san came to my office with another bundle of Sensei's old journals and magazines for me to look through and note the ones I want copied. He's forgotten I know the bit about the wrapping paper and told me again to leave them in their wrapping paper on his desk if he's not around. When he wears that "ingrown" look, he forgets I remember what he's told me about how to care for these very old papers and journals. Since his return from holidays spent at home, he's been carrying around weighty thoughts that may have to do with Sensei's rapidly declining health. If it's something more, something personal, he won't discuss it with me.

If Kenichi were here, he would tell me or at least allude to what's troubling Watanabe. If Kenichi were here, Sensei could relax about meeting the project's completion date. When I met Sensei in the hall today, his usual good spirits and resolute will were tempered by pain that made his face wince and his shoulders jerk forward ever so slightly.

Wednesday, January 13. Sensei is in the hospital. He's very sick according to Watanabe-san who doesn't look well himself as he has a very bad cold and wears a surgical mask to work. The mask warns people to keep their distance and not breach the modicum of personal space the mask provides. Whether it's his concern with Sensei's health or something else, a bad cold added to it makes him plainly miserable.

Friday, January 15. Today, when I took the articles I'd marked to Watanabe-san's office, Akuma told me Watanabe-san's father died Wednesday night and he'd left to take care of funeral arrangements. Watanabe-san is the older child and only son and is now responsible for his mother and younger sister whose wedding is to take place this spring. According to Akuma, family responsibilities could keep Watanabe-san away several weeks.

"You'll have to rely on me now," he said, gathering intention to strike a numbing blow. "I don't suppose you've heard...he (meaning Kenichi) won't be coming back to Kyoto. The Tokyo office cancelled his return. He won't need to climb into your bed now that he can hop on his wife every night."

Akuma has been waiting for an opportunity like this to spew venomous words at me for daring to rebuke him in a public place and in the presence of other men. Apparently, obscene remarks he hisses at me in the hallway aren't giving him the degree of satisfaction he craves. His human emotions had decayed to such an extent the smell of hate is unmistakable.

My mind reeled from the impact of that hate, but some self-protective instinct put my body in motion and spun me around and out of that room to send me fleeing down the hall to my office before he could strike again. I didn't stop to shut my door as I rushed in to collect books and materials to take home. I sat down at my desk and was bending over to look in a bottom drawer for a shopping bag I'd stored there when he rushed in kicking the door shut behind him. Before I could move, he was leaning over me with one hand on the opposite arm of my chair and the other on the backrest to prevent me from standing up.

Hot cigarette breath covered my cheek as he hissed, "You're nothing but a foreign whore, and he's thrown you away just like all the other women he uses and discards." He rubbed his hand over my breasts adding spitefully, "I've felt bigger tits on Japanese women" and was out of the office as quickly as he had come in.

113

I turned cold and began to shake. I pulled at my blouse as if that could push away the impression of his hand on me. I had to get to safety before I broke down completely. I don't remember walking home or up the stairs to my apartment, but I did lock the door behind me before I sank to the floor and cried.

I got up when my ribcage ached from sobbing and crawled into bed with my clothes on. I fell asleep sooner than I would have supposed and woke just as it was getting dark. I made a cup of tea I drank in bed wrapped in the green quilt. Later, while standing in a hot shower scrubbing away hate and ugliness, anger came to my defense and took away my need to cry.

<u>Late Sunday, January 17</u>. Yesterday morning was cold and damp; a gray blanket of clouds covered the mountains. I settled in on the sofa with a cup of tea and journal articles I wanted to read. I was determined not to spend the day wondering how I was going to safely manage the rest of the year on my own. If Akuma is right about Kenichi not returning to Kyoto, since his home office does have the right to cancel his remaining time here, Kenichi, I'm sure, will contact me...eventually.

Akuma is jealous of Kenichi's aplomb in wooing and winning the woman he wants, while he, Akuma, has to take unwilling women by stealth and force or pay money for their submission. He planned his revenge well, much better than his plan to get away with groping my leg under the table. With no other man around to deter his hate-filled behavior, he gets away with groping me and spewing poisonous venom in my ear.

As far as I know, nothing can be done about Akuma's behavior, at least not legally. He's counting on my reluctance to discuss a matter like this with Sensei because Sensei is now too weakened by illness to take on further responsibility for Akuma's behavior. Akuma can feel secure in leaving the result of his assault entirely with me.

The telephone rang. Joy of joys, it was Kenichi!

I was surprised and started to cry, "Oh, Kenichi, Akuma told me you were not coming back. He said your Tokyo office wouldn't let you return."

"Akuma doesn't know beans about what I'm doing. Marina, what's wrong? Are you all right? You're crying."

"You came back early because of Sensei?"

"Yes, Watanabe-san and I have stayed in touch. I got in late Friday afternoon and spent the evening and this morning at the hospital with Sensei and Mrs. Hiraizumi. He's determined to get better, and I think it's possible he might. Let's not waste time. I'll tell you everything when I see you. Will you meet me at Demachi-Yanagi train station at two o'clock? I know a quiet inn on the mountain where we can spend the night."

The train was not crowded. We sat apart from other passengers and concealed the hands we were holding between us on the seat.

"What did you do while I was away?" he asked studying my face.

"I sent an application to a women's college near Philadelphia. I had a long talk with Dr. Smith about the position, and she thinks I'm the right person for the job. The problem is the college wants someone with more teaching experience and publications. Since I began working on the translation, I haven't thought much about writing anything else."

"This is the time to work on the translation. What else?"

"I couldn't stop thinking about you."

"I thought about you in the wine I drank, in the furniture I used... it was impossible to stop thinking about you."

"Why do you tell me this in a public place? I want to touch you, and I can't, not while we're on a train."

"When we get to the inn, I'll repeat what I said and you can touch me wherever it pleases you."

We erupted in laughter, causing heads to turn in our direction. It was marvelous to feel humor and joy reenter my life.

When we stepped down from the train at the mountain stop, a blast of cold, raw air made me gasp. Kenichi said we should take a taxi to the inn, although he had told me on the train it wasn't far from the station.

"Let's walk," I said. "We've had to share the first minutes of our reunion with other passengers on the train, and I don't want to share more time with a taxi driver."

We walked up the narrow street leading up the hill away from the small cluster of lighted shops and restaurants near the train stop. We turned left at the top of the street onto a quiet, deserted road leading farther up the hill to the inn. We were alone in the cold, damp mountain air. The houses we passed were hidden behind well-made fences. There was no one around to be curious about us. Kenichi pulled me to him and kissed me.

"This is happiness," I said, putting my arms more tightly around his neck and returning his kiss.

He lifted me up by the waist and swung me around. "Love...love," was what he told the uninterested world around us.

We pressed against each other as we resumed our walk. I've missed being physically close to him.

Perched on the mountain and shrouded in mist, the Inn of the Two Doves appears to be quite small, but the full extent of the building is hidden by architectural design. There were several pairs of shoes in the *genkan* shoebox, yet we saw no other guests in the halls we traveled and heard only a low murmur of voices coming from one room we passed. Following the maid along this winding series of passageways was all that was necessary to make me think we were leaving the rest of the world behind.

Moments after the maid who had escorted us to our room bowed her way out, another maid appeared with tea. I was shivering from both the cold and the excitement of being with Kenichi again. He asked her to let us know as soon as our private bath was ready.

While we were soaking in deep hot water, he asked, "Why are you smiling?"

"I was wondering if anyone has ever been hard-boiled while taking an *ofuro*."

"You are warm now, aren't you?"

"Yes. Do you think our meeting this year is unfortunate?"

"Why unfortunate?"

"Because we are happy together and have so little time in which to enjoy each other."

"We are happy together, and we do have time to enjoy each other. Think of it that way."

Later, as we were finishing dinner in our room, he reached across the table to take my hand. "What happened while I was away?"

"Sensei was hospitalized for another round of cancer treatment, and Watanabe-san's father died."

"You know I don't mean that. Tell me what's happened to you. You are holding onto something I can't decipher by myself. I want all of you with me tonight, not just 85 or 90 percent, so tell me."

He didn't expect it to be what I did tell him about Akuma taking revenge for being publicly rebuked.

Kenichi became very still, very quiet. Then he said, "Marina, I will take care of this matter in my own way and time. It may take longer than you would like, but I promise you, I will take care of this. You will know I've kept my promise."

"But, what...?"

"No more about this tonight," he added brightly and kissed my hand. "Let me take care of it as I have promised to do. If we forget Akuma for the time being, we won't give him the satisfaction of spoiling our reunion. We can be alone."

After the dishes and remains of our meal were cleared away and our two futons were laid side by side, we stretched out and continued to talk.

"I once read in an old book that Japanese people think kissing is unclean. Do you think it is?" I asked.

"No."

"Do you kiss the people you love often?"

He chuckled. "Think about it, Marina. Do I?"

"Yes, and I like it very much."

He lay over on his back, and I traced the lobe of his ear with my finger. "This is the Buddha lobe, isn't it? Your lobe is not as large as those I've seen on Buddhist images. If you were a Buddha, you wouldn't be thinking about making love to me."

He turned and smiled. "How is it you know what I am thinking?"

"It's elementary, my dear Kenichi; we share the same heart. Your princely profile goes well with your noble character."

He took my hand roughly in his. "Don't delude yourself; I'm not as noble as you like to think."

"You are my ideal man because we can talk about everything. You share your heart with me and that makes you and our conversation very special."

"I want to please you, but that doesn't make me noble. Someday, you'll meet a truly noble and generous man and you'll know what real nobility is. I envy that man and what he'll find with you."

"I don't think it's possible to love another man the way I love you. No other man is as interesting or as attractive or as wonderful as you are, no matter how generous and noble his character."

"What can I say to that?"

"There is nothing to say. We've used our quota of unnecessary words, and now we have to act."

"I agree."

We were laughing as we reached for each other.

Thursday, January 21. Dear Diary, I am in love—capital **L** capital **O** capital **V** capital **E**. How is it that I have lived so long without a love that moves my heart in such exquisite turns? I marvel at the radiant, happy woman I see in the mirror. She asks, "Why probe this new sense of wholeness when you know you're incapable of reducing loving and being loved by Kenichi to words?" She's an image of understanding because she knows I want to preserve what I can of these precious days in my diary.

When I was little and was told I had my grandfather's brown eyes, my father's smile, and my mother's thick hair, I studied my face in a mirror. Where was the authentic "I" among all the traits passed on to me through my family?

When we were teenagers, my girlfriends and I studied our images in mirrors to see how we looked to the world of boys. In the mirror I'm using now, I see happiness, lovely, lovely happiness. I'm not really beautiful, but the way my body, the way my mind and heart respond to Kenichi's love has made me so.

Our lovemaking is blissful; in the exquisite, timeless moments we share, we are indivisibly one, not separate people. Can two separate people really become one, or is it only momentary forgetfulness? Loving him gives me an experience of timelessness where nothing is broken, separated from its source of joy, divided, fragmented, or incomplete. The oneness in our lovemaking is another reminder of paradise.

Late at night, the bedroom is lit by lights from the street below as well as beams of headlights that skate across the wall whenever a car comes up Higashioji Street. When I sat back on the bed with part of the green quilt wrapped around my folded legs, he told me my body was luminous, like a lotus blossom. He told me the love I have brought him dispels the darkness he sometimes feels. He says loving me deepens his joy in the inexplicable.

I told him with a sweep of my arms that loving him helps me see beyond heaven's closed gate, that I could see Paradise with the eyes of my heart.

He laughed and told me I had developed an extraordinary talent and to please not let the public know or a curious crowd would expect me to turn water into sake. We laughed as we rolled back together to find more down-to-earth pleasures in loving each other.

Thursday, February 11. When it's possible to spend an evening in my apartment and not just a good part of the night, we prepare a light supper together. He makes a better cup of instant coffee than I do because he has the patience to wait until the boiling water calms down before pouring it slowly over the freeze-dried granules. Some time during the evening, while I'm working at the table and he's stretched out on the sofa reading, he gets up to make tea and lightly touches my neck or bends down to kiss me as he walks by. It makes these rare evenings together extraordinary.

He's going to Tokyo this weekend for the first time since his return here in January. While he's away, I'll spend far too much time thinking about the hunger that marks our lovemaking when he returns. I don't have to consult the calendar to know this Kyoto paradise will be sealed off without hope of return when I leave for California.

Last night, after he had turned over on his side away from me to sleep, I told him, "I want to stay in Japan with you."

Alert, he turned around to face me. "Do you mean it? Are you sure? You may still hear from that women's college in Pennsylvania."

"It's been too long; if they were really interested in interviewing me, they would have let me know by now. Would you be willing to live these next weeks with the idea of my staying here? We have to talk about the pros and cons. I need to know if I'm capable of living in Tokyo where I won't be able to forget I have to share you with your family and long hours required by your job."

"I know someone who could help you find a position at a women's college in Tokyo. Haruko knows the Tokyo real-estate market inside and out; she would help us find an apartment you could make a comfortable home."

"There will be problems," I said, wondering how I would break the news to my parents who were counting on my return in June. Kyoto I can manage on my own, but Tokyo, I'm not sure. I would need to find a close circle of friends to offset the loneliness a large city stirs up in me, and I want an expanse of natural, uncluttered space around me. Where would I find that in Tokyo? I'd miss California's trees and wooded mountains, the rugged coastline—all that scenic beauty never far away.

As we lay back on opposite sides of the bed to stare at the ceiling, Kenichi echoed my concern when he said, "There will be problems."

Saturday, February 13. A first! Kenichi called me from Tokyo "to talk."

I dreaded hearing the real reason for his call and asked, "Are you coming back?"

"Yes, I'll be with you tomorrow night. I called to hear the sound of your voice."

Does being with his family make him doubt what he has found with me? Does he think I'm something he conjured up to fill an empty chamber in his many-chambered heart?

"Oh, Kenichi, I am not something you dreamed up. I am real. I love you. I want you here with me. I ache with longing while you're away."

It must be difficult for both of them when he does go home. There is no way she cannot know what has been happening in Kyoto. She's lived with him long enough to know when his mind is occupied with another woman. She has had two children with him, shared years of everyday life, and put energy into making their marriage a success. She would know when his heart opens to thoughts about another woman.

She's intelligent, a keen observer and reader of his moods and thoughts. She would have been concerned, if not alarmed, when she realized he was having sex with women he met at Haruko's parties. She would have read signs of inattention before they ever got around to talking about it, if they ever did or do talk about it. It must have been devastating when she realized I had become more to him than a casual affair. Are they relying on the language of habit to communicate their intention of staying together?

He depends on her unstinted support, her understanding and willingness to help with his responsibilities at work and as head of their extended family. He loves her as well as me, but she must doubt this now because of what she sees in him when he first steps into their house after spending weeks in Kyoto with me. It would wound her to think his *joie de vivre* has more to do with me than her. She loves and wants him or she wouldn't be able to endure self-doubt and their current state of tension. Maybe she's waiting to see whether or not I decide to stay in Japan.

While Kenichi and I were talking on the telephone, I wanted to tell him to come back and stay here until May when his work here ends. I know he won't do it because he misses his children. He doesn't want this disruption with his wife to affect his sons' schoolwork and their chances of being admitted to a good university. He wants them to know they can rely on him, and to do this, he has to return to Tokyo as often as possible to stay involved.

If I do leave Japan, where will our love go? What if his longing for me overtakes him at work? Will he pretend to read an office memo while trying to hold on to the remembrance of me? When he stops in at Trina's gallery to have lunch or tea, will he envy the fact she and Shuji share their daily life, and we never will?

After I leave, if I do leave, he's sure to attend another of Haruko's parties where he could meet one of the women with whom he once played. His good manners, easy charm, and sense of humor will help smooth their way through what could otherwise be a stilted conversation. If she alludes to the possibility of playing together again, will he pursue her knowing he won't feel the love that he says now makes him feel he's one of the blessed?

Will the love we've shared, the love we may be forced by circumstances to leave behind, cause him to ponder our brief season of indescribable states? I think about our separation when he sings *"The Way You Look Tonight,"* another favorite by Jerome Kern and Dorothy Fields.

Sunday, February 27. We were lying in bed behind the half-drawn curtain listening to the trolley coming up Higashioji Street and rumbling to a stop near the apartment building. I was in his arms with my head resting on his chest listening to his heartbeat and waiting for the sneeze and swoosh that announce the trolley's readiness to move on before clicking contentedly past the apartment building to gain necessary speed to reach Hyakumanben trolley stop. I was remembering how the trolley swayed from side to side when I sensed Kenichi had opened his heart to thoughts about his wife. I sat up and backed onto the green quilt.

I watched him a moment before saying, "You're thinking about your wife."

He sat up, placing pillows behind his back and covering himself with the sheet. "Ours was an arranged marriage, and we've made a success of it. This you know. You also know I do not want to lose what she and I have built together for our sons. This is not the place to discuss my marriage, but if you have a question that needs answering, I will hear it and decide if it is something I want to answer."

"I have no question."

"Then I want to talk about things I find easier to say when the shadows in this room lower my inhibitions about talking about myself. Loving you as I do has made it possible to tell you things I've never been able to say to anyone else.

"That first night—do you remember? You had just washed your hair. I was intoxicated with the scent of your hair, with you. Cascades of your hair covered both of us with the scent of flowers and indescribable happiness. I marveled at the fearlessness with which you loved me. I was surprised by love, too surprised to register its impact until later while we were dancing together.

"Life has been good to me, Marina, very good. I've been able to get whatever I've wanted without giving away too much of myself. When I was younger and more confident in my ability to command and control, I considered poetry an intellectual word game, a technical feat I could master with the right teacher and my own perseverance. I learned the best of my country's poetry and literature and made these concepts and worded insights my own.

"Until you, I hadn't found it necessary to search the heavens for words to describe my love for a woman. It wasn't until we made love the first time that I understood the heart I had guarded so well limited the depth and resonance of the poetry I read and wrote...and how I've loved the people who mean so much to me.

"If you do decide to stay, I can't promise the life the two of us will build together in Tokyo will be easy or satisfying for you. We already know the obstacles to our seeing each other every day. The disappointments that come along could cause you to regret your decision to stay...."

He did not continue, and we did not speak as we moved back together and stretched out side by side. He pulled the sheet and comforter over both of us and said no more.

Thursday, March 18. Last month, I didn't have one possibility of a job in the States, and now, for the past two weeks, I've been considering two positions. It's encouraging to know in spite of what I have been reading in academic journals about fewer jobs being available; there may still be one for me at home.

The first offer came from the coed college in the Midwest. I answered their ad last fall and didn't expect to hear more after they sent a formal acknowledgement and thank you. I considered the Midwest a possibility last year when I was susceptible to thinking I had abandoned my career for this chance to work in Kyoto. Things have changed since then, and my thinking about where I want to work has also changed.

My intuitive response to this offer didn't jibe with the map since my intuition tells me the Midwest is farther from California than the East Coast. Intuition is accurate in this particular case because if the job didn't turn out to be as satisfying as my next job needs to be in order to survive my separation from Kenichi, it would heap misery on my head to start another job search so soon after moving back to the States. I would regret not having stayed in Japan. I would want to return to Tokyo and find solace with him, and that would be impossible as there can be no hope of our being reunited after I leave here. I sent that college a letter of sincere thanks along with my regrets.

The second offer of an interview comes from Pennsylvania's College for Women, a smaller school not far from Philadelphia. It's the job I want, the one I've hoped would be mine someday, the one I'm willing to do whatever I need to do in order to win the position and keep it. However slight the possibility of getting this job, it's a way of shoring up my heart when I think about leaving him. Being invited to interview and lecture has a face-saving quality when I talk with Sensei or Watanabe-san about the history of the area and using my study of *Mountain Temple Woman* in my lecture.

The PCW Chair was candid about my chances. She told me the committee has already interviewed several well-qualified applicants, and I keenly felt her emphasis on "well-qualified." Dr. Smith persuaded the department chair (add a blast of trumpets here!) to hold a spot for me as the last candidate they will interview before making their final decision. They set my interview date in early June, which means I won't be able to stay in Japan throughout the summer.

My telephone conversations with Dr. Smith remind me of the several trips we made to the campus coffee shop when she had fifteen minutes or a half hour to talk with me about my thesis. I have missed that kind of attentive, energetic, and forthright female companionship here. It's one of the many things I hope to find at Pennsylvania's College for Women if I am selected for the position.

Mother told me in a recent phone call and then repeated it in a letter she mailed the same day that I should take the job at PCW if it's offered, that I mustn't think taking a job in California would please them more. Anywhere I decide to live in the US will be okay with them; Pennsylvania sounds good. She said she'd checked with the airlines and Pennsylvania is a five- or six-hour flight from California depending on the tailwind, maybe it was headwind, and she and Dad would visit me as often as possible, this from a woman who has never been on an airplane and has never wanted to leave California because it had, until this possibility opened, everything she wanted.

If I do not get the job at PCW, I know my parents will help me get through my disappointment and rev up for a future round of applications and interviews.

I used to think California was the only place for me, but now I'm thinking PENNSYLVANIA! Perhaps a long time ago, at least sometime after 1670, one of my ancestors might have traveled to Pennsylvania. As far-fetched as this may be, it does make Pennsylvania more friendly and more of a possibility. However slight my chances are, the prospect gives me hope of making a life for myself in the States.

I haven't the slightest chance of getting what I really want, that is to marry Kenichi and live with him the rest of my life. I want to be his official and only wife, not the unofficial second one. I am the woman, who for love of this man was ready to cut another pattern from the original design for my career in order to be with him, BUT we cannot marry and that is what I want. If we had the slightest possibility of that, I would stay.

We cannot have children. Kenichi says we can, and he would welcome another child, but I do not want to have children unless we can live together and he comes home to us every night.

He is pained by this kind of talk, and I am pained when we don't talk about it. It's an anguish that has left us standing in the living room holding each other and crying. I am relentless and will continue to be relentless when it comes to examining the position I would occupy on his wife's home turf. My close proximity to her would cause tension, no matter how sprawling that city is. Her relatives and friends could assemble formidable opposition to my hope for a quiet, untroubled life with Kenichi; after all, he is her husband however much I would like to forget it.

The emotional and physical needs of two households quartered in the same city would strain his ability to be a master of both. When he returns to the Agency for Cultural Affairs and the job that rightfully claims the majority of his time, he will be mired again in a bureaucracy that leaves little time for two families. When would he find time for himself away from his job, his family, and me? He does need occasional respites from a job that can be tedious, mundane, and overlaid and undermined by bureaucratic mediocrity. Where could he go to be alone and rest without adding to the concern of the two households who cherish him?

A big city like Tokyo would be less of a problem for me if we could live together, if I could see him every day. No matter how comfortable I made my apartment there, his infrequent visits would make the city colder and lonelier; unbearable is the word that comes to mind.

Also, if I turned down the interview at PCW to stay here, could I live with the possibility the job could have been mine, would have been mine if I had returned to the States for the interview? The job I have always wanted, the job I have worked for is not available in Japan. If I stayed here, would rehashing my decision not to leave make me resentful or bitter? Would I end up lamenting how the world has passed me by?

These questions I ask myself, these questions I ask him: "How can I live without you? How is it going to be possible?"

I am working on my lecture. I've amassed several pages of notes now spread over the dining room table. I want to focus on the woman's life, citing the fact she had to learn as we all do how to rally her strengths and depend on herself to manage her successes, however small, as well as a range of personal disappointments or whatever else came along to test her perseverance, her patience and determination, and her knowledge of herself. I also want to mention her love affairs, the interweaving Buddhist thought, the historical period, and one or two passages that illustrate her daily practice of paying attention.

To mention all this falls a tad short of my reading the whole translation and would only make my audience restless; besides, they will be able to read it in its entirety when it's published. Right now, I have to pare away the unnecessary and come up with a core that will interest people who re-examine life and its possibilities when they reflect on the lives and the choices characters make in books they read.

<u>Monday, April 19</u>. By holding onto each other, we somehow got past the decision I had to make without being completely overwhelmed by it. Working steadily on my lecture and completing the translation helps me forget we have little more than a month and a half to be together.

When I saw a newspaper photo of a plum tree in bloom, I didn't want to make a special trip to see another reminder of how quickly time is passing. I didn't have to. During a solitary walk around the neighborhood, jutting up above a wall, the branch of a plum tree with fresh blossoms called my attention to this beautiful spring.

When the cherry trees blossomed in Heian Shrine Garden, Kenichi and I went to see them before he left to spend a week with his family. I went back to the garden by myself to stand inside the gate and linger with other spectators intent on taking pleasure in the sight. Cherry blossoms are actively beautiful in the way they collect the light and throw it out onto the rapt faces in the crowd watching pale pink petals float to the ground under those long hanging branches. The petals were as bright as sequins when they first touched the damp, dark earth under the tree. Petals that had fallen earlier, perhaps just that morning, were taking on the color of the soil to which they were returning.

Much has been written about the transitory, ephemeral life of these blossoms, but I was prompted by sunlight radiating through the bright blossoms clinging to the branches to pray, "Most merciful and compassionate God, grant me light to find my way."

After his release from the hospital, Sensei returned to campus to work in his office. Cancer continues to drain greater quantities of his strength, and he spends several days at home in order to work a few hours at the university. He is more wasted than I want to see. I guess I'd been hoping his self-discipline and formidable will would defeat the disease. Reports about his health change from day to day, the day after I heard discouraging news, I saw him in his office busy with work. Kenichi or Watanabe-san will take the final portion of my translation to his house as soon as I am finished with it, then I'll wait until he feels well enough to arrange a meeting in the tearoom.

I am living my own version of the woman's preparation to leave the city for an uncertain future. The tile roofs in my neighborhood are still close at hand, and the mountains are distant in my perspective. Papers and books are scattered across the dining room table. I stop to thumb through the portion of a book I was too sleepy to read last night and must read today. On the coffee table, yesterday's newspaper covers the book of poetry Kenichi and I have been reading together.

I think about him while I make the bed. How will I live without hope of seeing him again? What will I do with my love for him? Will it wither away like cherry blossoms or will it become an incurable longing I carry to my grave? I don't want to be disabled by loneliness when I return to the States or become so devoted to memory I get mired in the past. I want the kind of clarity the woman was seeking. I don't want to live a solitary life in the States, but I am returning to one when I leave here.

Monday, April 26. Watanabe-san called me at home this morning to say Sensei wanted to meet me in the teashop at 11:30.

Sensei is very thin, but while we're talking, I forget he is ill. His voice and more exactly, the discipline and practice supporting his words convey an impressively strong presence. The waitress brought *sencha* in cups resting on wooden saucers. He took a sip and motioned for me to do the same.

He told me my translation presents the woman as she was. There are no major problems that need immediate attention; however, he did ask me to consider waiting two or three years after I return to the States before attempting to publish my work.

"Why, Sensei, why wait three years?"

He took another sip of tea. "You will be adjusting to your new college and making new friends. You will be moving from a quiet, relatively reclusive and focused period of study to being actively involved with students and building your career. You will have responsibilities that will take time and thought, add to your pleasure, and test your patience. Be generous with yourself, and take the necessary time to adjust to these new requirements and circumstances.

"During this adjustment period, you could publish an article or two about your work in progress in appropriate journals. Within two or three years, when you think the time is right, begin preparing your translation for publication. Three hundred years passed after the nobleman completed his diary before it was discovered in the statue of Kannon. Your American audience can wait three years to read an English translation."

Watanabe-san was waiting at the curb near the door of the teashop to drive Sensei home. The car was spotlessly clean inside and out and had such a high polish I could clearly distinguish my reflection in the paint.

I walked home along Higashioji Street thinking about the advice Sensei offered to my waiting, listening mind. Three years from now, will my mind be less clouded by my love and longing for Kenichi? Will I be capable of rereading and rewriting portions of the woman's life without imposing memories of him on my work? Will I ever be able to give up wanting a happily-ever-after life with him?

Somewhere among Lady Murasaki's writings, she says it could possibly take three or four years for a broken heart to mend. She must have thought it would take that long for the shattered portion of the heart to have scarred over, not completely healed necessarily, but enough so that one could live without the daily consciousness of an open wound. Lady Murasaki, like Sensei, encourages patience, the willingness to wait and see, to let one's own timing and life experience bring understanding and recovery to the loss.

Even if I have to wait three years for my translation to be published, although I hope I don't, I know books find people they are meant for, however long it takes. Didn't I find *The Lady Who Loved Insects* when I needed her most, which was centuries after the story was written and several decades after Mr. Waley's translation had been published. The same holds true for *The Tale of Genji*.

Almost two years ago, when I visited Berkeley's East Asian library, I wasn't thinking about a year abroad, I was concerned about where I would teach after my contract with Southern Women's expired. When I opened the doors to the library, I wasn't expecting to find another door opening onto my future when I flipped through Asian art journals and was arrested in my tracks by the picture of the woman sitting on the porch of her hut.

My translation will find its audience, however small, after it's published. A curious historian may read it for the information it gives about ordinary life during an early period of Japanese history. It will appeal to someone interested in learning what an individual woman immersed in the social culture of her time could do and did with her limitations, possibilities, and choices. It may spur an attentive reader to formulate with greater accuracy what she has been searching for, what it is that moves her, what ideas or knowledge of herself have been directing her progress and development.

People who look to art as a guide or help in interpreting the meaning of life will appreciate the paintings in the nobleman's diary, which I hope will be reproduced in my published translation. Besides the springtime scene of the woman sitting on the porch of her hut, I like the one that depicts a sense of journey.

This picture shows her as a young woman standing alone on a small bridge in her father's well-maintained garden near their elaborate house or mansion. In the background, obscured a bit by clouds are the mountains and hills that make up Kyoto's surrounding landscape and, not to forget it, the area where she will eventually retire. She is not looking down at the water where carp gather expecting to be fed. She does not hide her face but looks directly, curiously at the viewer.

The artist's depiction of her standing alone and still on the highest arc of this artful bridge could be his rendering of the moment when she realizes her life is a journey. We know from the diary she's had to maneuver roadblocks and detours along the way, and, yes, cross many bridges before growing into the mature woman who made the choice of spending her remaining years near a temple in the hills.

Diary entries tell us after she first went to live near the temple, her adjustment to a more solitary life made her think loneliness would be an unending noise in her head, until the moment she heard crickets singing in the grass. At that moment, she realized her loneliness would come and go, just as crickets sing loudest in summer and die when the weather turns cold. She told the nobleman she had seen a version of her own life unfolding the day she watched a cicada that had recently emerged from the ground gradually unfold and straighten its legs before it could right itself and find its own voice.

Pictures and entries like these open our understanding of her life and journey.

Saturday, May 22. The other day, while I was packing books to mail home, we talked about taking a short trip together before we leave Kyoto. I did not want to go to a popular resort where, to avoid being stared at and commented on, we might feel restricted or confined to our room.

"I would like to take you to Ise Shrine," he said. "You've never been there, and I would like the two of us to see it together. It's been a long time since my parents took my sisters and me, and I would like to see it again. The giant cedars are magnificent; their foliage will remind you of California's giant sequoias. We can leave tomorrow and spend the next two days and nights together."

We left my apartment with its empty cartons and sealed boxes. We left Kyoto station and the backs of buildings and narrow porches with the morning's laundry strung on bamboo poles. We outdistanced a man on a bicycle balancing two crates of empty sake bottles strapped atop the rear wheel.

In the band of commercialism bordering Ise Shrine, there are carts, restaurants, and kiosks selling ice cream and soft drinks, as well as more typical Japanese snack foods such as dried squid and rice crackers and small pancakes stuffed with sweetened soybean jam. Tour buses stop in this area to unload large groups of visitors, each equipped with a camera, or so it seemed. They flock around souvenir and food stands, buy more film, and line up to use the public toilets.

The Isuzu River separates this band of commercialism from the primordial beauty within the shrine. On the other side of Uji Bridge, within the shrine precincts, there is an ablution site where visitors wash their hands and mouths as a token gesture of purification before starting out on a walk along the graveled paths.

What struck me first was how large and un-crowded, how magnificent the setting is in real life. The tourists walking around us could be forgotten in the space and silence beneath tall Japanese cedars and the sky overhead. During our slow walk, the natural simplicity in smooth stones, clear water, tall trees, and that great blue sky overhead helped me breathe more deeply and cleared my mind of superfluous thoughts. A magnificent cryptomeria tree belted with a sacred rope is perfectly situated in a setting like this. There is quiet order everywhere as well as a sense of cleanliness and purity. There even seems to be purity in the silence that was broken now and then when I became conscious of the crunching and grinding of people's shoes on the gravel paths.

The two main shrine buildings and the lesser shrines are enclosed behind a series of four fences, each with narrowing gaps between the posts. A visitor sees only the buildings' miscanthus reed thatched roofs and the ridge pole ornaments. The mystery of sacred architecture is mostly hidden from the general visitor, but it is possible to see how geometric space can be transformed into sacred space when dedicated rectangles and squares are purposefully outlined with single bands of wood (about the size of railroad ties) and the space within covered with a layer of small rocks. These now empty dedicated areas are silent reminders that new shrine buildings will be constructed there in the future.

Ise Shrine is rebuilt every twenty years. Two rectangular shrine compounds known as the eastern and western sectors are laid out side by side. When a new shrine building is erected on the eastern sector, the one on the western sector is removed. On the empty western sector, a small shed is built around the "heart pillar" of the building that has been taken down and removed. Twenty years later, when it is time to rebuild on the western sector, that heart pillar will be realigned before a new shrine building is constructed around it.

Kenichi told me the eastern sector had been empty except for the small shed around the heart pillar when he came here with his parents. As we stood before the now empty western sector, he linked my arm in his and held it against his body. He would not have touched me in a public place like this if he didn't consider us to be alone, and for that moment at least, he did not include the few people walking by on the wide path behind us.

"I am glad I could bring you here," was all he would say through the emotion he was trying hard to control.

That night, while we were eating supper in our room in a Japanese inn, I said, "I envy your wife and the meals she will share with you and your children. She knows she is fortunate to be married to a man with your qualities."

"Don't make yourself unhappy by thinking about these things. We knew from the beginning it would be impossible for us to marry."

"And it remains impossible, but I still want it."

"And I want it, too, Marina."

Later, we moved to a window where we watched low repetitive waves of water moving along next to a pedestrian walk with empty benches. I felt as though we had already moved to opposite sides of the ocean. I could not think of anything to say to bridge the distance between us.

He began, "When the shrine is rebuilt, the new thatch and the golden hue of the new wood reminds me of a rice harvest. In a wet climate like ours, it doesn't take long for moss to grow on the thatch and the wood to darken."

"Kenichi, please don't be obscure tonight. You know better than most how to woo with words. Just say plainly whatever it is you want to say; it's all my heart can bear."

"Do you remember the small shed protecting the heart pillar?"

"Yes."

"It was on the western sector."

"What?" I blurted out. "Are you telling me that if I wait patiently in America for twenty years, you will come to the States and I will see you again?"

"Marina, do not look at the time we will be apart, look at what we must do."

"Reconstruct?"

"Reconstruct."

"You may be able to realign your heart and rebuild your house, but I am incapable of loving anyone but you."

"Someday, you will find you want to love again. You'll want to have children and a family of your own."

"You say that because you have many loves, and I am only one of them. I want you, only you, and I will want you for the rest of my life. I'm going to cut my hair and become a nun."

"Oh, Marina." He was laughing now. "You will not become a nun." Then, more softly, "These past few months have been a paradise for me as well. Do you think I want you to leave…to never see you again? When you leave, you will be taking indescribable joy with you, leaving me desolate. It won't be easy to forget what we've known together. If you would let me be the flawed, earthly man I know myself to be, you would see more of my faults and weaknesses, you would know I will be yearning for you long after you have found someone else and learned to live without me. Even so, we will both learn to live without the other."

"But how? You keep saying we are going to, but you won't tell me how. I'll have to tear out my heart and all memory of you if I am to live without you."

"Oh, Marina, Marina," he said, pulling me into his arms. "I really don't know how. All I can tell you is that you—I—will know when it happens."

We held on to each other as if that could prevent our inevitable parting, but a few moments later, we relaxed and forgot everything except that we were together and we loved each other.

The next morning at breakfast, he asked if I wanted to visit the shrine again.

"No. You might find another lesson I don't want to learn."

We laughed and found other things in the area to see and do that took up what we considered a reasonable amount of time before we returned to the inn to enjoy more of the special pleasure we find in each other's arms.

<u>Tuesday, May 25</u>. Yesterday, before noon, we started on a walk to the Silver Pavilion and halfway there, decided we didn't want to spend our last day together walking around those familiar paths. We walked back to our favorite pork cutlet restaurant across the street from the university and did not go in because we had no appetite for food. I suggested we walk to the river, and before we reached Hyakumanben trolley stop, he said, "This is wasting our time. Let's go to your apartment. I have something I want to give you."

That something is a dainty gold ginkgo leaf complete with ribs and notch on a gold chain. He slipped it around my neck saying, "Know that I have loved you these past 250,000,000 years and will continue to love you throughout the next 250 million."

I said, "Know that I am with you in the wine you drink, the furniture you use, the posts that support the fence surrounding your house. When you see a black, red, or white oak or any other species of my family of trees, remember I love you, have loved you, and will continue to love you as long as there are oak trees on this earth."

I regretted not having found something special for him, something he would not have to leave with his wallet and keys on his dresser or on a bookshelf in his home where someone would see my choice and question why he found that particular volume interesting.

"Marina, you've given me a love I thought would never be mine."

We spent most of the night talking and laughing. We were awake before dawn to talk some more and did not get up to shower until 7:00. We had no appetite for the toast and coffee I made for breakfast. If we had all the time in the world to spend together, it would not be long enough. If I knew the vocabulary of angels, it would be inadequate for all I wanted to say.

At the door, we said I love you and not goodbye.

He left on the afternoon train to return to his family in Tokyo.

Wednesday, May 26. Sensei and I met at the teashop today for our "closing ceremony" and a farewell cup of tea. I gave him a pewter bowl made by a Williamsburg craftsman as my thank-you-for-all-your-generosity-and-help-this-year gift. I bought this bowl in a gift shop near Southern Women's when I was fairly certain we would be working together. Today, when he took the perfectly smooth, metal bowl out of the box with his thin, bony hands and set it on the table between us, the sturdiness of the bowl seemed to mock Sensei's frail body and poor health.

Sensei found something appropriate to say to fit the occasion; he always does. He made a speech, this being our closing ceremony, about strengthening our lives by supporting craftsmen who make traditional arts and crafts.

We said goodbye at the curb where Watanabe-san was waiting beside the immaculate and freshly polished car to drive Sensei home.

I walked to the Kamo River to work off my discomfort with feelings about the bowl. I wanted to distract myself from all negative thoughts and sat on an empty bench near the river where I watched water flowing under the bridge. I wondered what I was going to do by myself the day and a half I had to spend in Tokyo before my plane left. I had only the final meeting with the Asuka Foundation Representative to take up time. I didn't want to visit Trina's art gallery, although she has continued to invite me through Kenichi. I am not interested in art at the moment, and I don't feel up to making conversation just to pass the time. Besides, if I did see for myself how happy she is, I would be tempted to rethink my decision to leave.

I thought about visiting my old Tokyo neighborhood, but after a few years of exchanging New Year's cards with Mrs. Matsui, we lost touch. I don't know if she is well enough to be living by herself or even if she would want me to call on her. What would I do in that neighborhood besides have a brief conversation with the bread lady at the store where I used to buy fruit and snacks? I doubt if she would remember me, although she might if I mention the year and why I had lived in Mrs. Matsui's house. There are no old times to review and no shared experiences to recall, not really. I don't want to be reduced to hoping dear Mrs. Nagashima would come along to distract my pain with her own torrent of emotions.

Too much has changed since I was a college student gleaning my knowledge of love from books and hearsay and awkward dates with overly eager boys. I have no past in Tokyo, only Kyoto. Whether I live in California or Pennsylvania, when I think about Japan, it will be Kyoto I remember and the trolley clicking up Higashioji Street late at night, a bedroom lit by street lights and darkened by shadows, the green quilt, the Inn of the Two Doves, and a joyful, exuberant reunion that can never be duplicated, although that's exactly what I want most right now.

He recommended the hotel in Tokyo where I'm staying and knows when I'm most likely to be there. I want him to come to my room and hold me until I change my mind and decide to stay in Japan with him, or at least somewhere nearby. I fantasize about what will happen if he does come to my room and we make love. It's not going to happen. When we said "I love you" at the door of my apartment, we were really saying goodbye. From that moment on, even if we were to meet again on a familiar street in Kyoto, we could not fly into each other's arms and resume what we are struggling so hard to leave behind. Who wants to die such a painful death twice?

If he does want to see me again before I leave, it will probably be at the airport where he can wait behind a pillar or a rack of magazines to let his mind take in my actual departure. He can watch me board the plane before going to the window to watch it taxi down the runway and wait to lift off. Perhaps after I'm airborne, he will turn completely to the task of rebuilding his life with his family. Perhaps the cold realization he will never see me again has already settled in, and he has adjusted to it by burying his feelings for me. If this is true, going to the airport to verify my departure would erode the progress he's made since returning to Tokyo.

A glacier is forming around my heart; it's begun to freeze all hope of seeing him again but not the fact I love him.

Friday, May 28. He was waiting for me in the hallway outside the Asuka Foundation Office. We stepped closer to the wall where we could talk without someone bumping into us.

"How are you?" he asked, searching my face for the answer before looking at the ginkgo leaf around my neck.

"I'm fine. You?"

"Fine. You're leaving tomorrow?"

"Yes. Sensei told me you were going to England this summer."

"Yes. We leave in two weeks. Have you completed your lecture?"

"Yes. I think it's pretty solid, but I won't know for sure until I hear their response and take questions."

"If the job at Pennsylvania's College for Women turns out to be the one you want, I hope it will be yours."

"Thank you."

A group of people came down the hall and stopped near where we were standing to continue their conversation.

"It's time for my appointment."

"I must leave now as well. I wanted to say goodbye and wish you well."

We looked at each other. Kenichi rallied first, but his voice broke when he said, "Goodbye, Marina."

We smiled conspiratorially at his intended meaning.

"Goodbye, Kenichi."

"Have a safe journey, Marina."

And you, my love, may life continue to treat you well.

Afterward

It was rewarding to lecture to a group of attentive and curious students and faculty. Their interested questions added to my confidence—I could teach...I wanted to teach...I would find a place for myself in America. While three students and I were touring the library and campus, the Native American in our group reminded us the town's main street had been an Indian trail before it became a well-traveled coach circuit and eventually the main street. A fitting reminder I was walking again on my own historically familiar soil.

Pennsylvania's College for Women had everything I wanted: well-spoken students; an active, involved faculty; a good library; and it was located in a town with tree-lined streets and preserved historic sites. The Philadelphia airport was not far from town, and this would make it easier to pick up and drop off my parents when they flew here to visit me—if I got the job. Before I left campus to catch my return flight to California, the department chair told me I would hear from the committee within a week to ten days. It was a few hours short of ten days when she called to say the job was mine and a confirmation letter was in the mail.

I had flown straight to Philadelphia from Tokyo, touching down in L.A. to change planes and call my parents to announce, "The wanderer has returned." We had only minutes to talk about my upcoming interview at PCW. My short hair was going to tell my mother far more than I wanted to say about the past year in Kyoto.

After my appointment at the Asuka Foundation Office, I'd had my hair cut in the hotel salon. The head stylist took a long time unbraiding my hair and brushing through its length, asking me several times in both Japanese and English if this was what I really wanted. He spoke English very well but had a hard time understanding why I would want to cut my hair short. I told him I had a job interview and wanted to look stylish. His assistant brought me a cup of tea, and I was left alone to consider my decision before the stylist returned and asked again how short he should cut my hair. Then while those long strands were ceremoniously wrapped in white paper and carried to a back room, I walked over to a sink to have my shoulder-length bob washed.

On the plane leaving Haneda, I was caught between what I was leaving behind and the stability I wanted to find in a new job and place. What was going to happen when I wasn't strapped in a seat and flying thousands of feet above the earth? Could I resist indulging in *if only* or *what if* and keep focused on *what is*? Sensei did say, "…being human we are weak." What if longing overtook me in Red Oak, or when I moved and became a stranger in a strange town with no close friends? Loneliness could easily seduce me into indulging myself in memories.

At the San Francisco airport, I walked into my mother's open arms and buried my head on her shoulder to avoid looking into her face.

"When did you cut your hair, Marina?"

"Just before I left Tokyo."

"Your braids were beautiful."

"It was time to change."

"But so short...."

"It's easier to take care of—just wash and dry."

"You've lost weight."

"I'm fine, Mom. Don't worry. I walked a lot in Kyoto; it kept me trim."

There were tears in my father's eyes when I moved into his arms, then to Aunt Elizabeth who pulled me to her in a reassuring hug. Uncle Arthur gave me a quick hug, the only way he expresses the loving things he finds hard to say to anyone except Aunt Elizabeth. He has always been more comfortable in his role as commander of his reunited troop, and the day I returned to California, he led us all to the baggage claim.

Those first few days when being home felt new and strange in spite of its familiarity, my father asked about my work on the translation and more about finding my way around Kyoto, and my mother listened and weighed the import of my answers. She prepared our favorite meals while Dad and I set the table, picked fresh greens for salad, and made the dressing. She didn't question the time I spent in my room or why I took their car for long, solitary drives. She's too perceptive to be deluded into believing the heartache I was carrying was the worry of finding a job.

The first days after I returned, Dad and I sat in the backyard sometimes talking about tomatoes and lettuce, sometimes holding hands. When my father wants to express sympathy for something I can't discuss at the moment, he holds my hand. My mother was trying to connect the happy youthful daughter they had taken to the airport almost a year ago with the subdued adult stranger sitting in the backyard. When she came out to join us, she'd pat my head affectionately and say something about the copper highlights in my hair or that my hair was as thick as hers had been when she was my age.

Not long after I knew the job at PCW was mine, Mother and I were in my bedroom sorting through linens I would take to furnish my next apartment. She stood beside where I was sitting on the edge of the bed and touched my hair.

"He must have been a wonderful man, Marina."

"How do you know he was wonderful?"

"You would not have sacrificed your hair for anyone less."

"We'll never see each other again, and I still love him."

"I know," she said and held me while I wept.

Mother didn't need to ask his name, how we'd met, or how he earned his living. She didn't need to ask why we had to separate or why we could not marry or even if he was Japanese or why I loved him. She felt her job as the parent of a grown daughter was not to satisfy herself with intimate details of my affair but to support my recovery from loss, from suffering, and to help me however she could to reestablish myself in Pennsylvania. Besides, at that time, so soon after my return to the States, I wasn't ready to part with a single detail of the happiness I had known with him. It was up to me to learn how to manage loneliness by restricting recall of the life we'd shared; still, whenever an unscheduled image of Kenichi rose up in my heart, I fought another losing battle with grief.

My mother told me, "Let yourself grieve, remember only what's necessary until the suffering subsides, but don't indulge yourself as this will distract from the life you need to make for yourself in Pennsylvania."

Before I'd left Kyoto, Watanabe-san came to my office to say goodbye. He was in a chatty mode and had been ever since the date for his marriage had been set. I'd responded with nods and "Is that so?" or "Really?" It was all he needed or wanted from me; after all, it was his story he wanted to tell. I could understand why the woman he wanted to marry after meeting with her only three times did not hesitate or ask for more time when the go-between passed on to her and her family Watanabe-san's proposal of marriage.

Then, with gentlemanly ease, he escorted me to a campus entrance for an official goodbye. At the gate, I thanked him for his patience with my many requests and for his help in making my work on the translation a success. I said I would acknowledge his help in the published copy. He smiled when he said, "Even if it takes three hundred years to get your book published, I will be waiting at Kyoto University to receive the copy you've promised to send me." I gave him my address in California with the request he keep me informed about Sensei.

The letter from Watanabe-san came around Thanksgiving telling me Sensei had died in August. He enclosed a copy of the eulogies and remembrances Sensei's colleagues and former students collected and printed for private distribution. I read and reread what Kenichi wrote about his teacher, friend and mentor and mourned but not for Sensei, who seemed to know better than most of us how to maintain balance with one foot in this world and one in the next. I mourned for the loss of the full measure of joy I had known with Kenichi.

Late spring the following year, Watanabe-san sent me the catalogue of the exhibition of scrolls they had readied. An exhibition had been mounted in Kyoto to honor Sensei's scholarly contribution to the study of Japanese Buddhist art, as well as provide the public with an initial viewing of these rare scrolls. In the letter he sent with the catalogue, Watanabe-san let me know that with this gift, his final obligation as second-in-command-go-between had been fulfilled. He wrote, "It is now your turn, O'Brien-san, to publish your translation and send me the promised copy."

He added a personal note that told me he and his wife were comfortably settled in an apartment in Kyoto from which he commuted to campus by bus, and Akuma had left Kyoto to take a position in Hokkaido.

It was all I needed to know; Kenichi had dealt with Akuma in his own way and time as he had said he would. After we'd returned from the mountain inn, Kenichi had taken a superior tone when he spoke with Akuma. When I first noticed it, I thought it was similar to the tone the Ladies of the Bath used to address Mrs. Nagashima to keep her at the edge of the group. Akuma, however, was not to be isolated at the edge of the group; he was being pushed into leaving town. An official version would read something like this: Akuma betrayed the trust Sensei placed in him when he appointed him a member of their department and a representative of Kyoto University when he acted in a dishonourable and reprehensible manner toward a foreign guest of their department.

Who or what else played a part in separating Akuma from his position at the university, or how a face-saving transfer to Hokkaido had been managed, I'll never know. Kenichi wasn't actually an employee of the university and would have needed the consensus of other, more influential people to maneuver Akuma to a colder, harsher climate.

I felt sure that while Kenichi was in Kyoto to attend the opening of the exhibition, he let Watanabe-san know he wanted me to know Akuma had lost his position at the university. He wanted me to know he had fulfilled his promise, and, I think, upheld the honor and integrity of the university and most of all, Sensei.

I read Watanabe-san's letter several times before taking my translation out of the woven lacquered box Sensei had given me as a Christmas present. I read through those carefully typed pages until I stumbled over the woman's ambiguity about leaving the city and was caught again between the life I wanted to make with him and the one I was making for myself. I returned the lacquered box to the bottom drawer of my desk wondering how many more months or years it would take before I could read through the translation without being reminded of what I had left behind.

The partially furnished first-floor apartment I rented near PCW was in a large old house that had been subdivided into three apartments. What I did not realize when I signed the lease was how the trees along my side of the house blocked the sunlight and left the rooms in shadow most of the day.

When my parents came to visit, they brought with them a definition of home that included large rooms and many windows opened to natural light and a restorative view of gardens. They saw a disparity between the obvious pleasure I was taking in my regenerated career and the dark rooms where I spent too many hours by myself. To hear my mother tell it, I was made up of light and would not be fully restored until I lived in rooms that welcomed more light.

She suggested I look for another apartment with more windows and move before I began accumulating large pieces of furniture and appliances. Better yet, my father added, if I was as happy at PCW as I seemed to be and wanted to stay in Pennsylvania, I should consider investing in a house of my own. We spent time driving around town looking at houses and talking about whether this or that one would or would not be suitable for me. We walked through a model in the group of townhouses being built near the edge of town, but we could not find much to say except it was clean and new.

That fall and winter, I bought tickets to every open house sponsored by the local historical society and the town's Junior League. I walked through homes with period furniture and small alcoves so carefully and artfully arranged my imagination had no room to play. When I read through listings in the local paper, I called an agent for a walk-through to consider if I, with my personal history and preferences, could live and flourish in that particular arrangement of space. No house I saw held my interest for more than a day or two. The house I wanted, the one that wanted me, was waiting, but where?

My first Christmas in Red Oak after I returned from Japan was a turning point for me. I reveled in the large, comfortable, well-lighted rooms in our house and what I thought was an unusually bright sun for that time of year. Delicious meals, my parents' obvious pleasure and pride in presenting me again to their friends and merchants they had known most of their lives, talks with Aunt E. about Japanese art, and listening to Uncle Arthur's concerned frustration with the war in Vietnam all went into making that holiday unique. My heart brimmed with love for the family who provided me with a comfortable, stable home while I was growing up, and now I was calling Pennsylvania home as well. Before I fell asleep in my old bedroom, I thought about how Kenichi and I loved each other for what the other opened or brought to our individual lives. Life has been good to me as well because I was working at a job I loved and in a place I could call home.

After the holidays, when I returned to a town shrouded in foggy winter weather and walked through the dark rooms in my apartment to turn up the heat and unpack my suitcase in the bedroom, I had the feeling I was on the verge of a new era in my life. Somewhere in my mind, a door opened by itself, and I was moving toward the threshold of a well-lighted, indeterminable space and time. I pictured myself as Amaterasu, who after hiding herself in a cave, knows she is ready to take her first steps out of self-imposed darkness to enter a world brightened by the sunny expectation of a yet-to-be-determined period of personal growth and prosperity.

The day I found my house was the first warm Saturday in late February. I was propelled out of my apartment by a longing to be in the country. I wanted to leave behind everything that had to do with papers and midterms, a nagging concern about my neglected translation, and an ongoing debate about whether to spend a long or short summer vacation in California. I drove out of town accompanied by snatches of music from passing cars and the congestion of traffic heading toward the supermarket and the completion of other Saturday errands. Farther out of town, farms and fields spread out beside the road. Birds rather than cars dashed by and called out from branches and fences where they perched.

I drove along a broad two-lane highway following a fairly wide and not too deep, or so I guessed, river on my right. Traffic had thinned out to an occasional car, and I could safely slow down to steal glimpses of the river. Coming up on the left side of the highway was a wedding chapel set back from the road and picturesquely situated in front of a low, uneven hill clustered with rocks and patches of melting snow. On the right, a bit beyond Wayside Chapel was an iron truss bridge. The road leading across the bridge was appropriately named

Bridge Road. I turned onto it and slowed down to a crawl to watch sunlight playing on the water below.

On the other side of the river, Bridge Road continued straight ahead as a paved country road. I took an immediate right onto Henderson Farm Road, opting for the adventure I might find on a dirt road running parallel with the river I saw in snatches at the bottom of the hill.

The first house I passed was an abandoned fieldstone farmhouse set back about thirty or forty feet from the road and boarded up against intruders. Farther on, I drove past a wooden farmhouse with a weathered barn set much farther back from the road, and beyond that was the much larger property of another wooden farmhouse with a new barn, smaller outbuildings, several horses in a large corral, and cows penned near the barn. Henderson was the name on the mailbox beside the driveway, and there was a turnaround for explorers like me who didn't know the road ended at Henderson's farm. Henderson Farm Road was rather short on adventure, or so I thought at the time. I decided to see what I could see from this side of the river before heading home.

I drove back to the abandoned house and parked in the dirt driveway to the right of the house. Eastern red cedar trees grew beside the driveway in a long row that stretched back beyond the house toward the open fields. I'm fond of eastern red cedars, more juniper than true cedar, and not just because the wood is used to make school pencils. These particular trees had grown to a remarkable height and were lined up beside the driveway like sentinels left to guard an otherwise forsaken outpost.

I walked across the dirt road to look down the sloping hill at the river, which in the sunlight resembled a silver ribbon with loose, tumbling diamonds rolling about in small dazzling shapes and in larger, brilliant clusters. The swiftly moving water carried these dancing, brilliant shapes under the bridge and out of sight while more diamonds appeared to take their place. The air was luminous, awakening in me the earth's promise of renewal and longer days of sunlight. In a few weeks, the forsythia beside my apartment would bloom, trees would bud, and the grass on campus would be emerald green and need frequent mowing to keep it trim.

I turned around to look at the stone house. The brown and gray earth-colored stones were soothing to my eyes after staring too long at diamonds tumbling on the water. Pulled closer by curiosity, I walked through the gate of a low stone fence into a yard cluttered with patches of snow covering dried leaves and twigs, fragments of newspaper, broken boards, scraps of faded wallpaper, and an empty soda can. The wrought-iron gate was bent and partially buried under a mound of dirt, snow, and miscellaneous trash.

I walked around the house hoping to find a window with a loose board I could pull away to have a look at the rooms inside. The storm shutters had been removed, but overall, the house was impressive. Obviously, someone had planned and built this house with forethought and care. Behind the house and directly up against one side of the first floor was a large wooden lean-to, for what purpose I didn't know. I found a warped board I pulled partially away and glimpsed the darkness inside. Whoever had sealed the house shut had done a thorough job.

There was another driveway on the left side of the house that was wide enough to accommodate a tractor or a team of horses pulling a hay wagon. This utility driveway led farther back behind the house to the stone foundation of what was once a barn. Whoever had taken the shutters from the house must have carted away the barn's framing and lumber to sell or use in another building. I walked up the gradual incline into the open barn space for a better look around.

Parallel with the continuation of Bridge Road, a dense screen of eastern red cedars obscured fleeting glimpses of the farmhouse by cars passing by. Those tall trees were the right height for the sound of wind blowing through their branches to enter an open bedroom window and clear the mind of someone waiting to fall asleep.

Three redbud trees grew alongside the barn's stone foundation and could be seen from the back windows of the house. The blossoms are what distinguish these trees. In the wild, at least in California, some redbuds grow more like bushes than trees.

The fields behind the house lay fallow under large patches of melting snow, and beyond them were other farmhouses and fields. If the empty fields belonged to the stone house, I would re-forest them. Trees would channel rainwater and cool the air in summer and provide a home for birds and other small animals that would help regenerate these acres with seeds or nuts they dropped or buried. Trees would add a naturally dense and decorative screen for my property and another perspective to the flat, open fields along this side of Bridge Road. More importantly, at this unsteady point in my emotional life, I needed to pay attention to seasonal changes in trees around me and those I intended to plant and take the moments of reflection they offered. If I owned this house, I would put my heart into restoring it and the land belonging to it. This was the house I wanted, the one that wanted me.

I drove back to Mrs. Henderson's to ask about the stone house. She told me she had inherited the property from a great aunt over thirty years ago. The house was in a sad state then and has deteriorated through neglect to its present shell. She'd listed the house with a realtor, but no buyer was interested after seeing its impoverished condition. To earn some money from the house, Mrs. Henderson's son had sold the kitchen cabinets, doors, shutters, and the barn to a used lumber liquidator. She gave me the name of the realtor who might still have the listing in her retired file. Using a shortcut Mrs. Henderson traced on my map, I clocked the hour and fifteen minutes it took to drive back to PCW on a good day.

I needed an architect, a knowledgeable, thorough craftsman to help me realize my hopes for the house, someone who would understand my wanting to be on site whenever possible to learn all I could about the details and process of making this house my home. Just as importantly, I wanted to keep the natural world close to the center of my home by making the windows large enough to bring in views of the river, the surrounding farmland, the eastern red cedar and redbud trees, and the variety of other trees I intended to plant on the empty fields behind my house. The lean-to at the back of the house gave me the idea of adding a glass-enclosed room, a solarium of sorts where I could read, look at a full moon, gage the growth of my reforestation project, or just assess the amount of snow I would have to deal with in order to get to work.

A colleague recommended the architect who had renovated her historic house ten years earlier. She had been the first client of the man and wife who had just opened their firm. A few years later, she read in the newspaper that the young woman had died.

The architects helped my colleague discover the original dimensions of her house by taking down a wall beside the kitchen fireplace that hid a narrow stairwell to a second-floor bedroom. The door at the top of the stairwell had also been boarded up and hidden behind parcel board, plaster, and layers of wallpaper. In a drawer built into the top step of the stairwell, they found a wooden box with a daybook belonging to the original owners of the house. Distinct handwriting styles led my friend to think both the husband and wife kept track of the names of their houseguests, the dates they visited and for how long, as well as daily expenditures and notes about their children's illnesses and the weather.

The rediscovery of spaces that have been blocked or hidden for a period of time makes a fascinating story. Rehabilitating a house that held my imagination could help me stay focused in the present. Getting involved with the restoration could help me learn to carry the past more lightly.

During my first telephone conversation with Edward Boatwright, he told me he knew where Bridge Road was because he drove by it while he had been working at another site. He'd noticed the stone house on the hill and thought about stopping and exploring its possibilities but had been too busy at the time to do so. We set a time to meet at the house.

I arrived early that day in order to walk around the house and through it to look for anything I might have forgotten to include in the list of changes I wanted to discuss with Mr. Boatwright. I stood for a moment on the road in front of my house to look across the river at the cars pulling up in front of Wayside Chapel. A woman dressed in white and carrying a short bridal veil stepped from a car. The weather was clear and sunny, a perfect day for a wedding.

I turned away to admire the single row of eastern red cedars beside the driveway. When the property was surveyed, I was happy to learn these trees grew on my land. If they belonged to my neighbor, I would have derived continuous pleasure from the sight of them, but the fact they grew on my property gave them a positive role in the restoration of the house, if only by their example of constancy.

A hollow, unpainted front door had replaced the original one. It had swollen and dried so often over the years it now took a great deal of pushing and shoving to get it open. The first time the realtor and I went into the house, we weren't able to see very well because she'd removed boards from only one window. (Later, she'd tell me she expected me to walk out as quickly as other prospective buyers had.) Luckily, we both brought flashlights because I intended to walk through the entire house. The basic structure of the house was sound, and when I entered the empty, desolate rooms, my imagination opened a store of possibilities.

The day the architect and I were to meet, there were no boarded windows. With more light, I could see the nest field mice had made in the large stone fireplace on the left wall of the living room and the partial skeleton of a bird unable to make its return flight up and out of the chimney and in another corner, the desiccated remains of a squirrel. There was nothing to see under a broken floorboard except a scattering of small stones since the house didn't have a basement. The living and dining rooms would be opened into one very large generous room and the whole house warmed by central heating. Only a freestanding sink with a rusted hand pump was left in the kitchen. Faint outlines on the wall told the story of cupboards that had been removed and carted away. It was a large room with plenty of space for appliances, a heater or furnace, and a small powder room near the mudroom.

The two bedrooms on the second floor directly above the living-dining room opened awkwardly into one another. I planned to live here by myself so this dividing wall would be removed to make a combination bedroom-study for me. Another large-sized bedroom across the hallway from mine and directly over the kitchen would make a comfortable room for my parents or Aunt E. and Uncle A. whenever they came to visit.

There was space in the wide hallway closet between these two bedrooms to add a full bathroom. The stairwell banister and rails were oak, as were the cupboards and drawers along the side wall. The wood was undamaged and removing neglect would restore its patina. The front hallway window offered a good view of the river, the bridge, and Wayside Chapel. Near this window is a stairwell to an attic only high enough to bend over and push a box or boxes along. It wasn't my grandmother's attic.

I returned to the living room and slumped down on the sturdy crate the real-estate agent left after I told her I wanted to buy the house. Wayside Chapel's bell began ringing out the good news of the man and woman who moments before had promised to take the other as their lawfully wedded husband or wife.

The two of us stood in the hallway outside the Asuka Foundation Office to voice our intentions:

"Goodbye, Kenichi."

"Goodbye, Marina. Have a safe journey."

I touched the gingko necklace and began to cry. Buying this house and putting down roots in America was taking me farther than the plane ride across the Pacific. When I stopped crying, my denim shirt looked as if I'd been standing in a shower. I wiped my eyes on my sleeves and walked to the open door to let the air dry my shirt while I looked for the green truck the architect said he would be driving. Edward Boatwright was standing in the utility driveway beside the truck. It didn't take genius to figure out he had walked up to the door, heard me crying, and had gone back to wait beside his truck.

I crossed my arms over my body to cover my shirt and wet sleeves, but as he walked along the road and entered through the gate, my hands dropped. It wasn't necessary to hide, explain, or apologize to someone who was giving me time to collect myself by following the designated path to my door rather than jumping over the low fence and cutting across the yard.

He held out his hand as he introduced himself. I put mine into his and looked into sapphire blue eyes set in a surprisingly handsome face before stepping back into the house to let him enter. We walked through various rooms talking about possibilities. Edward suggested adding another observation room outside my bedroom-study directly above the one I wanted on the first floor. He suggested turning the attic into a third floor by lifting the roof several feet. It would be divided into two rooms: a small narrow one over the far end of my study to be used for storage and the larger room finished off as another bedroom if or when my parents or Aunt E. came to live with me. A bathroom would also be added to this bedroom.

There was much to like in Edward's careful and appreciative assessment of the original builder's skill with wood and stone. I liked the attention he paid to my concerns and hopes for the house and the direct way he stated why things could or couldn't be done and where a substitute or perhaps a compromise could help me reach my desired goal. He raised no objection to my dropping by to observe work in progress, as I knew to be cautious on a worksite.

After he'd finished drawing preliminary plans, we met at my campus office to go over them together. And later, while we were eating lunch in the faculty cafe, I told him about my grandfather, the house he built, and favorite pieces of furniture he'd made for my grandmother.

Dramatic phases of the restoration began for me with the re-digging of the well and the gutting of the house. It was not as ceremonious as I imagined the realigning of a heart pillar would be, as the restoration of my house was probably more messy, but I felt a noticeable degree of joy when fresh water was located and tapped, and when large portions of old flooring were being replaced, I clearly saw the ground on which my house is built. As old plaster was removed from the wall, and windows on the ground floor enlarged, the stale odor in these neglected rooms floated out of the empty shell along with some of the dust.

Learning about electrical outlets, central heating, pine board versus hardwood flooring, and plumbing fixtures and deciding on the exact shade of green tile for the bathrooms kept me interested and involved in each phase. While I was driving back to my apartment or while I was putting food in my apartment refrigerator or drinking tea before settling down to write a lecture or correct term papers, I thought about what I was learning about the art and craft of house building. In this and in other less obvious and unexplainable ways, being present during the restoration of my house kept me focused on what I was learning and discovering in Pennsylvania.

Even with thirty cartons of books and a forgotten number of other boxes of various sizes and dimensions stacked in the middle of the living room, my new house felt the most empty the day I moved in. As usual, there were more boxes of books than furniture to move from apartment to truck and truck to house and only my bedroom and the kitchen could have been described as furnished. The two students I paid to help me load and unload the truck claimed this had been one of their easiest moves.

After we returned the empty U-Haul and had eaten dinner at a restaurant near the main highway before saying goodnight, I drove back to my house listening to but not hearing a summary of national news and the local weather report. When I turned onto Bridge Road and crossed the river, I saw a cold moon hanging over my house and thought it to be like the Star of Bethlehem. That star directed seekers to the place where hope was reborn and where the sweet breath of compassion and mercy mingled with the warm breath of animals, the fragrant smell of clean hay, and a mother's concern for her newborn's safety and well-being.

I went into the house giving thanks for central heating and into the kitchen to marvel again at the newness of it all. I leaned on the jelly cupboard, the first large piece of furniture my grandfather made when he was a boy. He'd used wood from crates that had been used to ship laundry soap on the railroad; the unpainted back of the jelly cupboard names Chicago, St. Louis, and Omaha.

My student helpers had brought chocolate cake to snack on while we were unloading the truck. I took the last piece of cake up to my room on one of the *Imari* plates my mother discovered in the attic while she was sorting through my grandmother's large accumulation of goods. Neither Mother nor Aunt E. remembered my grandmother using these plates, which is not surprising since she did not appreciate Oriental design, Oriental anything. They reasoned that one of the many guests my grandparents entertained, most likely out-of-towners who did not know my grandmother's tastes, had given her this boxed set of plates as a thank-you gift. Never intending to use them, she took the box up to the attic and stored it in a larger box before placing it behind a tall stack of heavier boxes she rarely moved.

I stood for a moment with my cake at the top of the stairs to admire the banister and wall of cupboards. Depending on the time of day and the angle and amount of sunlight coming through the hall window, the patina of the wood rises and deepens. As on other particularly moving occasions, the warmth and beauty of wood brings my family to mind. Moving into my own house was another major step toward a more independent adult life; it made me grateful for my family's help in reaching this stage of my life.

My great-grandfather made the washstand in my bedroom from boards of black willow a new farmer in Red Oak had given him in exchange for the loan of a plow horse. The farmer may have given more in trade but only the washstand remains to validate the story. The jelly cupboard, washstand, and the solid cherry bedstead and dresser my parents bought for me when I outgrew my child's bed were the first pieces of furniture to be shipped from Red Oak to help furnish my new home.

The lights next to my bed can be dimmed to ease me into a restful night's sleep, while those in my study brighten my desk and the overstuffed chair and ottoman where I can read late into the night. I had shelved five cartons of the ten my helpers and I carried up to my room earlier that day. Ten boxes were all I could manage to look at without feeling overwhelmed by the task of having to shelve all thirty.

I hung the vertical scroll Aunt Elizabeth sent me as a housewarming gift. In 1956, she'd taken me with her to Mr. Tanaka's shop of affordable (at least for Americans) treasures. Way back then, there was much less traffic, and getting around by car was the best way for someone as determined as Aunt E to find out-of-the-way places that sold woodblock prints, hanging scrolls, and old pottery.

There was nothing Ginza-like in the area of Mr. Tanaka's shop, no bustle or neon lights to identify a store where Americans were welcomed. Aunt E. parked the car on a wide street, and we walked to a narrow lane that led us through a quiet Japanese neighborhood with houses hidden behind tall fences and closed gates. Mr. Tanaka's store was farther up this lane and more obviously a place of business with its frosted-glass sliding doors just a step across the covered drainage ditch that ran the length of the street.

We left our shoes on the *genkan's* cement floor and stepped up onto the *tatami* to sit on cushions around a low table. In the time it took for our eyes to adjust to the dim interior, Mrs. Tanaka appeared with tea, bowed her head in welcome, and placed our cups on the table. She bowed again before she disappeared behind the curtain that separated the shop from their living quarters.

We drank tea while Aunt E. and Mr. Tanaka talked (in both English and Japanese) about the hot weather and the fact that I was a high school student and visiting Japan for the first time that summer. While Mr. Tanaka was bringing out the various things he wanted to show Aunt E., she would turn to me now and then to interpret a word or two, leaving the Japanese portion of what was being said for after our return to the street. I wasn't especially interested in the scrolls with landscapes of mountains and lakes and tiny people seated in pavilions or boats that Mr. Tanaka hung for Aunt's inspection. My eyes wandered around the room until they settled on storage jars enrobed in shadowy seclusion provided by a deep shelf.

I snapped to attention when Mr. Tanaka hung the scroll of a gardener wearing a short, Japanese-style jacket, pants rolled up to his knees, and straw sandals on his feet. The gardener's jacket was colored with blue wash, his pants were a light charcoal wash, and there were traces of green on the leaves of the two slender bushes that had roots rounded up in balls of burlap, ready for transplanting. The gardener was sweeping the ground with a twig broom (sweeping away illusions, Aunt would later tell me). The painter's brush strokes captured the round, joyful face of the gardener to make this scroll attractive and alive.

In 1956, I had been pleased when Aunt E. bought this scroll. I was even more pleased in 1973 when she sent it to me as a housewarming gift.

On another wall in my study, I hung a reproduction of the most familiar painting from the nobleman's diary, the picture Sensei used to illustrate the article that had gotten me interested in working on a translation. He had given me his copy of the picture during our leave-taking ceremony. When I untied its cloth wrapping and saw the picture, my eyes had filled with tears. I was touched and reached for his hand resting on the table.

He patted my hand in return, a fatherly gesture, and said, "O'Brien-san, be strong. Draw on your inner strength, and you will find your way."

I stood close to the painting to study how well the artist used delicate strokes to define trees and mountains, the distant pagoda, the woman's kimono, and lines that added years to her face. I stretched out on my bed and continued to think about the picture. It may have been the distance between my bed and the painting that started me thinking the woman could have been considering the potential in the open landscape around her, the potential in relocating to the mountains some distance from the heat and activity in the city... from Kyoto to the mountains...from Kyoto to Pennsylvania...from heartbreak to a potentially happier life.

It may have been thoughts about potential that jumpstarted me into reviewing my translation and getting it ready to send to a publisher. Permission to reproduce the paintings delayed its publication another four months. It was almost three years after I left Kyoto before I could send the promised copy to Watanabe-san. I dedicated the book to Sensei.

If during a telephone conversation with Watanabe-san, Kenichi learned my translation had been published or during a chance look-see in Tokyo's Kinokuniya bookstore he would read my acknowledgement of his help and know affection infused those few plain words.

The woods behind my house developed with the help of other people and of course, Mother Nature. After the land was surveyed, I followed the line of stakes outlining my property until I was fairly certain where I would begin planting the variety of trees that now grow there. As soon as weather permitted, I planted a male ginkgo tree at the edge of the woods I see from my house. Once in awhile, I'd walk out to the ginkgo to look more closely at its dark green fan-shaped leaves, but as things got busy, I forgot about it. By the time I moved into the house in November, the branches were as bare as a skeleton.

I planted two cryptomeria trees and discovered I liked watching their long hanging foliage sway back and forth in the wind like the long sleeves on an unmarried woman's kimono. When my parents visited, my father planted two northern red oak seedlings he had grown from acorns. Edward's nieces and nephews heard about my forestry project and sent a lunch bag of acorns they'd gathered.

Months before the house was ready, I had scrambled down the hill across the road from the house to have a closer look at the river, which was deeper than I had originally thought and treacherous where the hill dropped abruptly into the swiftly flowing water. During the climb back up the hill, I wondered if Japanese cherry trees would survive on this rather precarious slope. They did. The three I planted across the wide hill have not grown very large. They do offer a welcoming sight in spring when I drive home across the bridge. If I am fortunate enough to be standing on the road or looking out a window and see wind scattering cherry petals over the hill and the river, I am a willing hostage of that particular moment.

Then, too, there is the moon, always the moon, so unusually large and full. After I moved into the house, it filled the solarium near my bedroom with its white light and drew me from my bed to sit and marvel and think about nothing in particular until Edward came to mind. I could see his blue eyes and his dark hair and how it curled in humid weather and hear him laughing when something delighted him. Once I saw him halt abruptly, stand very still, and hold the piece of lumber in his hands with such tenderness, I thought a loving memory of his wife must surely have overtaken him.

The restoration of my house brought us together, and it was the interest and receptivity we sensed in each other during the walk through that made it clear we shared more of life than house building. When the house was almost finished and we were seeing less of each other because he was spending more time working on new projects, he called me or I called him because our longing to share the day with an understanding friend drew us to the phone. It was all so natural and so necessary to be together.

Thanksgiving Day, the day after I moved into the house, we drove to his sister's home for dinner with his family. Edward's parents had been killed in an automobile accident when he was sixteen, and his aunt watched over him and his younger sister while their elder sister was away at college.

Edward met the girl he would marry while they were both in graduate school. They married after graduation and opened their firm with a single client—the woman who recommended his work to me. During the second year of their marriage, his wife was diagnosed with breast cancer they thought would be cured by surgery, but five years later, another more aggressive brain tumor took her life. Two years later, he married again, too hastily they both discovered, and within a year, they agreed to divorce.

When I did not volunteer a similar kind of personal history, he asked, "What about you? What can you tell me about the man who made you cry the day we met at your house?"

"How do you know I wasn't feeling sorry for myself? The house was a disaster."

"I recognize grief when I hear it."

"He and I were perfect together. We were unable to marry."

"He was married. (It was a statement, not a question.) If he had been free to marry, he wouldn't have let you go. Do you still love him?"

"Yes. I always will in one way or another. It's probably not so different from the way you still love your wife."

"My wife and I had a special song, *'When I Fall in Love, It will be Forever,'* by Edward Heyman and Victor Young. Are you familiar with the lyrics? Seven years was all the time we had together, and seven years wasn't my...our definition of forever."

The following spring, Edward brought a dogwood tree to plant in the woods (the first of several he would plant), carrying it to up to my front door as he might a large bouquet. Surprised and pleased, I leaned against the doorjamb and smiled at him across the blossoms he was using to partially cover his face. Trees have a way of exposing our feelings to light and air, whether or not we are willing to voice them, and I wondered if Edward was aware of what his heart, hidden among those few blossoms, revealed?

I loved him, not as a young girl loves for the first time, but as a woman ready to explore the potential beyond the idealized love I kept frozen in ice around my heart. How could we, or would we, find a way past loss and be able to give ourselves to each other?

I wanted to rebuild the barn and include a small, self-sufficient apartment with the idea of persuading both my parents and Aunt E. and Uncle A. to move in with me when the time was right. Plus, the amount of snow last winter had already persuaded me to build a garage or a barn for my car. It would never be a barn in the way I intended to use it, but I wanted it to look like one. Edward came to my house to discuss preliminary plans. When he got up from the sofa to call his office, he stood in the kitchen doorway with his back pressed against the jamb and his head down over the phone waiting for his secretary to come back to the phone with the information he had asked her to find.

I was sitting on the sofa looking over brochures about a conference in San Francisco I planned to attend before spending a couple of weeks in Red Oak, but as I watched Edward's long legs move under his jeans when he adjusted his position in the doorway, I lost interest in the conference. I imagined holding him in my arms and my hands moving across his back. Heat radiated from my body, and I reached up to touch the perspiration collecting on the back of my neck near my hairline. It made me laugh.

"What's so funny?" Edward wanted to know as he hung up the phone.

"The glacier is melting."

"Is that a Zen *koan* you learned in Japan?" he asked from the doorway.

"Something like that," was all I managed to say because I couldn't stop beaming at him.

He watched me from the doorway a few seconds before walking over to the sofa in a few quick strides and bending down to kiss me. I reached up with open arms to receive and return his kiss.

We had three weeks before we left for San Francisco to talk about what we hoped to bring to our marriage and what we wanted from it and many other things besides the vows we intended to make to each other.

As soon as we got off the plane in California, Aunt E. and Uncle A. drove us to the office of the Clerk of the Circuit Court to apply for a marriage license and then to have the required blood tests. After I finished with necessary conference meetings, the four of us drove up to Red Oak. Edward and I were married in Red Oak Presbyterian Church with my parents, Aunt. E., Uncle A., and a small group of friends and relatives to witness our vows and enjoy a reception afterwards at home. I wore my mother's wedding dress, my grandmother's emerald and diamond jewelry, and a crown of fresh flowers on my head in place of the crown of braids I once intended to wear.

We both wanted children as soon as possible. Eleven months after we were married, Julian Edward was born. We were delirious with joy, although some delirium was probably caused by lack of sleep and new-parent anxiety. Eighteen months later, we welcomed John Arthur. Words cannot describe our happiness or the pleasure we derived from cradling our infant sons in our arms, their recognition of us, their eagerness to explore and learn, their first teeth, their first steps, their first words, and on and on. A great many new parents share a version of this ode to joy and add verses of their own making to this old hymn to new life.

Some years later, during a wave of increased ardor, I realized love had been working throughout the earliest years of our marriage and family life to clear my mind of dusty cobwebs, dispel shadows, and open blocked passageways to light. The love I shared with Kenichi had become part of my personal history and did not have the power to limit the full life I was building with Edward.

My parents came to Pennsylvania every year to spend three or four weeks with us, and we made California a large part of and sometimes our only vacation. Shortly after we returned home from one of these visits, Mother called to tell us Uncle Arthur had died. I couldn't believe it. I had taken his robust, healthy appearance and the fact he ate a healthy diet and exercised regularly as a guarantee he would live at least thirty more years. During our most recent visit, when the boys commented on how fast he had walked them to a restaurant open for breakfast before the rest of the town heard reveille, I was convinced Uncle Arthur would have a long life.

About six years later, my parents died within five months of each other. They, too, were in good health except for a few aches and pains. Two weeks before my father died, he told my mother he felt more tired than usual. The doctor could find nothing wrong. Usually, an afternoon nap reenergized him, but one afternoon, he did not wake up. After his death, my mother would not spend more than two weeks at a time in Pennsylvania because Red Oak was where she felt the most content. I could understand her wanting to be home where she felt my father's presence in the rooms of their house, but my heart froze when she talked about not wanting him to leave Red Oak without her.

Her next-door neighbor checked on her every day, but telephone calls with the neighbor and my mother were not enough to allay my apprehension. I decided to spend a month in Red Oak where I could watch over her, and the boys could distract her from thoughts about joining my father. Before the children's school was dismissed for the summer, Mother's neighbor called to tell me she had found my mother dead in the chair where she had been reading.

To people who attended her funeral and expressed their regret or stopped by with food they'd prepared for our meals, I could not say much more than thank you. I don't remember her funeral very well because disbelief and grief were compounded by the recent death of my father and the loss of my childhood surety. I did see what a trooper Aunt Elizabeth was when her own heart was breaking. I remember Edward standing next to me at the church and cemetery and shaking hands with a long line of people who came to express their sympathy.

Later that same summer, I took Julian and John back to California to help me clear out the house before it was put up for sale. Aunt Elizabeth came to help with stories about growing up in Red Oak, and both my sons and I learned more about their grandparents and great-grandparents.

John called Aunt Elizabeth's recollections "delicious talk" because of the way she described making homemade ice cream with ripe peaches or strawberries at family reunions; the mayonnaise with parsley, chives, and tarragon my grandmother added to egg salad; the lemons that had to be squeezed, sweetened, and iced to make lemonade; and those first mouth-watering bites of coconut cake or banana cream pie at church socials. John got the idea his grandmother and Aunt Elizabeth had been pioneers after Aunt E. told him how the old back porch steamed with hot water and the smell of laundry soap when they bent over a tub of hot water and used a rubbing board to remove dirt and stains from soiled clothing. Way back then, she told the small boy whose mouth opened in wonder, women used the power of the sun to bleach towels, bedding, and diapers, often spreading them over bushes and on the grass when there wasn't enough room on the clothesline to hang them to dry.

During an afternoon walk to buy ice cream, I thought about how my once small hometown had been and still is active in the making of American history. During the 1930s, two farm families left the dust bowl in Oklahoma to settle on two acres near Red Oak and worked hard to buy land and more land until their holdings spread out toward the mountains. Now their children and grandchildren were selling this land to a developer eager to house Red Oak's rapidly increasing population. During World War II and after, the town assimilated mostly Polish, Armenian, and Chinese refugees. Since then, the majority of immigrants have come from Mexico, Korea, India, and the Middle East.

My grandfather served on several committees during World War I and throughout the Depression. Other committees were added during the Second World War, and many of these were disbanded after the war. Since then, local and federal governments have stepped in with necessary services until the listing of numbers to call when help is needed now fills three and a half pages of Red Oak's expanding telephone directory. The hospital began with ten beds after the diphtheria epidemic, now it has 120 beds.

When my father worked as a postman, he walked from the post office throughout the neighborhoods where he delivered mail and greeted by name all the women at home waiting for their mail. Mail is now brought to neighborhoods in small trucks and often pushed along sidewalks in carts because the amount of junk mail, mail-order catalogues, and packages delivered by the post office has greatly increased the weight.

Because memories are more difficult to remove than varnish, it took several years after the death of my parents before I could sort through things I had shipped back to Pennsylvania and stored in the barn. Precious items such as the sideboard my grandfather made from black walnut found a place of honor in our house as soon as it arrived from California. My grandmother's trunk of linens, something I've treasured and wanted for my own, had been shipped to my house on Henderson Farm Road the year I moved in. Although Julian and John were young when their grandparents died, they each claimed pieces of their furniture while we were clearing out the house. They may think differently about their selections when they are older and have developed other tastes or stronger preferences, but in the meantime, this furniture remains in the barn waiting to be claimed.

Mother started clearing out the attic in earnest after I married. For all the happiness she expressed about my marriage, it made her realize life was moving on, and I probably wouldn't be moving back to California. The attic wasn't her main occupation, and it took several years to reduce the number of boxes. While we were vacationing in California, I cleared out the seven or eight I'd stored there.

Without stacks of boxes and the birdcage, the empty attic was just that—empty. Stripped of its mystery and power to enchant, the ancestors who once visited me in my dreams would feel dismay at the emptying out of that crowded room of family memories. My ancestors have never been able to confine themselves to sheets of graceful handwriting or the attic, however large, familiar, and comfortable it was while we all lived in the house. They would be dismayed when they came down the attic steps expecting to visit us in our dreams and found only empty rooms and no imagination to accommodate their presence. They had to come east and live with me because they would not find a place in the dreams of strangers who bought the house.

During the return flight to Pennsylvania, I distracted myself from thoughts about my parents and grandparents by picturing my ancestors bumping along on the boxes in the moving van heading east, discussing as they once had on the ship that brought them to America hundreds of year before what they might possibly find at the end of another long and uncomfortable trip.

Now my ancestors are pleased to be settled in the barn among a reduced number of packing boxes, although they do wonder at the lack of cows and horses, and they miss the smell of fresh hay that rightfully belongs in a building called a barn. They have adjusted and now appreciate the fact they are much closer to the East Coast where they disembarked hundreds of years before. When they go over to the Henderson's barn to appreciate authentic barn smells, the Henderson's ancestors tell them about people still coming from Europe and the now United Kingdom as well as Asia, Mexico, Central America, and the Middle East to build productive lives here.

At night, when my ancestors float through the house to look at the sideboard, the jelly cupboard, and the dishes that once graced my grandmother and mother's cupboards, they admire the central hallway of polished oak and appreciate what Edward and I have done and are doing to restore the house and land. At night, they look in on us being restored by sound sleep before they gather in the woods behind the house to give thanks for having found this new home in America.

When Aunt Elizabeth decided her house in San Francisco was too large to manage on a reduced amount of physical energy, we asked her again to come and live with us, but she said our house was too far from the bay to suit her. "A one-bedroom apartment is the halfway house I need to get used to living with fewer possessions. There's a family hotel nearby with a large swimming pool you'll enjoy when you come to visit."

She sent us things she wouldn't be using in her apartment in an assisted-living residence where two of her close friends also lived. While I was rearranging kitchen cupboards to make room for some of Aunt E's Japanese dishes, I picked up the blue and white cup I had bought in Kyoto during a lunch hour with Kenichi. Seeing it at that moment among everyday ware made me think about how time and experience have loosened and distilled the emotional impact on my memory of that lunch hour. Those first months after I moved into the apartment near campus, I inhaled the memory of the day I bought this cup along with the fragrance of the tea I was drinking. It was a significant moment for me in my house on Henderson Farm Road when I realized the memory of where and with whom I bought it could be recalled without anchoring the fullness of my affection in the past.

I went up to the attic to find my Kyoto diaries in the box of notes and papers I'd used while translating *Mountain Temple Woman*. I'd wrapped the diaries in the bamboo-patterned cloth Sensei had used to wrap the picture he presented to me during our leave-taking. I sat on the floor to read about the first time I fell in love.

Perhaps the work I put into translating the woman's life into modern English had more of an impact on my decision to leave Japan than I could recognize at the time. The woman's decision to leave the city came partly from her understanding of the limited options available to her, and that is true of me as well. Perhaps while I was writing out her experiences after she moved to the hills outside Kyoto, I had taken in the possibility that at some unspecified time in the future, I, too, might have occasion to review my earlier life.

Long before I starting working on the translation, the women in my family had been tutoring me about the need to reevaluate experience and memory. They gave time and attention to arranging and rearranging treasured belongings along with memories endowed to each piece and placed in storage what they could not bear to part with until some future time called it to mind when it could be reevaluated with the benefit of recently gained clarity.

I replaced my diaries in the box and walked down the attic steps through the bedroom to stand in the hallway where the heart of this house glows with the aid of the sun, then on down to the living room thinking about how the house and our individual lives have altered to accommodate family life. We had very little furniture when we married, and that was just as well since the empty space filled rather quickly with toys, trucks, and tricycles. The house now looks well used and comfortable, but not overcrowded with things we've bought to supplement the furniture and other things my parents and Aunt Elizabeth have given us.

The driveway beside the kitchen was leveled and blacktopped when we bought the boys pedal cars and roller skates. When they began using the driveway to play hockey and basketball, we parked our cars in the utility driveway.

The apartment in the barn became another office for Edward on the days he was home to watch the boys or to meet their school bus, and the children relished playing on swings he hung from rafters and making hideouts and forts and inventing games with the boxes stored there. When they were about four and six, they told us they wanted to live in the barn because they thought living in a house was boring.

The bedroom the boys shared across the hall from us had a high ceiling as there was no attic over that room, and Edward suggested putting in sleeping lofts to replace their beds and using the entire floor space for play. It was an interesting idea but not as appealing as living in the barn with swings, boxes, and hideouts. On a rainy afternoon during a game of hide-and-seek, the boys discovered, so to speak, the empty room we've continued to call the attic because it made the room special when all four of us camped there on family nights. Edward got them involved in designing the bedroom they've shared, and again some years later to accommodate their interests in computers and electronics, architecture, and science.

As I age, the thought that death will separate Edward and me someday comes to mind unbidden and unwelcomed, yet accepted as fact. I don't have to look at the Japanese cherry trees on the hill, the dogwoods that are Edward's favorite, redbuds, ginkgo, cryptomeria, pear and apple trees we've planted, eastern red cedars on both sides of our house, and our sons, once described by Uncle Arthur as saplings, to know as long as there are trees, I want to continue making my life with Edward and the family we share.

Acknowledgements

Thanks and appreciation to Yasuko Shimizu for suggestions, corrections, and encouragement after reading an early version of the Kyoto diary.

Mrs. Ota for guiding me to areas of Kyoto not always delineated on city maps.

Robert Margolis, Research Librarian, who found books I needed for background reading and research, sometimes before I realized I needed them.

Margaret Rich, Reference Librarian, Firestone Library, for finding the Arthur Waley Estate address after I got lost on the internet.

And especially Lady Murasaki who reached me through Arthur Waley's translation of *The Tale of Genji* on a summer afternoon in the 1970's, and left me awed with the scope of her talent, and with questions to resolve through study and writing.

About the Author

The author lives in Princeton, New Jersey.

Printed in the United States
56440LVS00004B/68